SINFULLY *Scandalous* MYSTERIES

Join Sinfully Scandalous readers everywhere and receive a FREE copy of Deadly Sins II: A Dezeray Jackson Mini-Series.

Visit www.koridmiller.com

North Downing: A Dezeray Jackson Novel

Sinfully Scandalous Mysteries, Volume 2

Kori D. Miller

Published by Back Porch Writer Press, 2016.

This is a work of fiction. Similarities to real people, places, or events are entirely coincidental.

NORTH DOWNING: A DEZERAY JACKSON NOVEL

First edition. April 30, 2016.

ISBN: 978-0991475681

Written by Kori D. Miller.

Also by Kori D. Miller

A Dezeray Jackson Short Read
Deadly Sins I
Deadly Sins II
Deadly Sins III

Sinfully Scandalous Mysteries
Hush: A Dezeray Jackson Novel
North Downing: A Dezeray Jackson Novel
Tempus: A Dezeray Jackson Novel

Standalone
My Life in Black and White

Watch for more at https://www.koridmiller.com.

"Melodies are just honest. They can only be what they are. Words have the capacity for deception. They're full of subtext, and some of them are cliché and overused and vernacular. They're tricky. All I can say is, words are tricky."

~ ANDREW BIRD

CHAPTER ONE

JAMES KEENEY ENTERED the six-foot -by nine-foot, white-walled room wearing the traditional khaki attire. His lanky frame didn't fill out his state-issued shirt, and the extra fabric of his pants gathered around his ankles. I waited near a rectangular, wood table with four chairs, two on each side. Keeney's crooked smile revealed the yellowed teeth of a long-time smoker. The door made a noticeable *click* when it shut behind him. That was always unnerving. Being locked inside the Nebraska State Penitentiary in Lincoln, NE, even if it's as a visitor, has never been on my bucket list. I could see the back of the officer's head through the small window in the door as he moved away. Keeney pulled out one of the chairs, his back to the door, and sat. I took the seat opposite his, opened a small notebook, and waited for him to start talking. It was Wednesday morning, and to be honest, I wasn't in the mood to talk with Keeney, but I felt sorry for him.

"Thanks for meetin me. I didn't think ya would." His Southern drawl was more pronounced than I remembered.

"What's this about, Keeney?"

He took a deep breath and leaned back in his chair, propping his left arm on the back of it, and smoothed his goatee. His hair had whitened since I last saw him. He leaned forward, resting his right hand on top of the table.

"Seriously, Keeney, I don't have all day."

"They wanna string me up for a murder."

"What?"

"Yeah. Me. A murder."

"Whose murder?"

"Some chick named Bridgeton."

"Bridgeton? You're going to have to give me a little bit more to go on."

"Sarah Mathews Bridgeton."

I shook my head. The name seemed familiar, but I couldn't place it.

"Someone, not me, killed her about a year before you got to Omaha."

"And you know her because?"

"I may or may not have burglarized her house."

I pushed back from the table, ready to go.

"Wait!" Keeney reached for my hand, then thinking better of it, pulled it back. Probably remembering the beatdown I gave him when we met.

"You gotta help me. I didn't do it. I mean, yeah, maybe I was there, but I didn't kill her. She was dead when I got in. Or nearly, anyway."

I stared at him for a beat, trying to recall what made me decide to accept his request for a visit. Dark circles formed around his droopy eyes.

"Look, Ms. Jackson, I ain't got no one else who can help me. I got some shit for brains PD. That's all, and he looks like he'll piss his pants in front of the judge. Besides, I ain't done nothin. Not this time."

"What do you expect me to do, Keeney?"

"You know, do your thing. You're a PI. Do some PI shit."

"PI shit?"

"You know what I mean. I need your help. And I can pay ya."

"Really? With what, stolen jewelry?"

"Nah. I got money. Go see my girl, Mazy. She's in South O, off of Twenty-fourth and Vinton." He gave me the address. "Will ya help me?"

That was the million-dollar question. It was more like "should I?" I had a soft spot for this piece of shit, two-bit burglar, and I couldn't explain why, but did I want to spend my time doing his public defender's job? And what about his PD? They have people who can do this crap for them. I noticed Keeney was staring at me, still expecting an answer.

"Well, will ya?"

"Yeah, I'll help you, but you're paying my usual rate."

"No problem. I gotchya covered." He held up three fingers on his left hand.

"It's the other hand, dumbass," I said, and stood to leave. Keeney screeched his chair back and stood.

"Thanks, Ms. Jackson."

AFTER LEAVING THE PEN, I headed to Yia Yia's pizza on "O" Street for a few quick slices before heading back to the office. I was still standing in for my former colleague, Haithem Nazari, at Tracer International. For a Wednesday, the lunch crowd seemed sparse, but I wasn't going to complain. Thirty minutes later, and with my stomach satisfied, I ordered a few of Dalton's favorites "to go" and returned to the office.

Guards greeted me as I entered the building. I approached their large round desk to sign in. The guard station was a new addition to the main entrance.

"Is that Yia Yia's?" one of them asked.

"Yep."

"Damn. Now I want pizza. My wife's gonna be pissed if I come home with a full lunch box, though," he said.

"Maybe you should rethink the pizza, then. Getting on the wrong side of your wife sounds like a bad plan," I said.

"No doubt," he said, and waved me past the recently installed gates.

After Haithem disappeared, the company higher-ups decided to strengthen the visible security presence in the building. He wasn't taken from here, but they wanted the staff to feel more at ease.

"Have a good afternoon, Ms. Jackson," he said, as I disappeared behind the elevator doors.

Dalton was waiting for me when I exited the elevator on Haithem's floor. He had a habit of doing this, and I couldn't figure out how he knew when I was coming. I'd started making it a game, varying when I'd leave and return, but he always seemed to know.

"The security desk calls you, don't they?" I said, as the doors closed behind me.

"Ms. Jackson?"

"Never mind. What do you have for me on Keeney?" I'd sent Dalton a text message while I was eating lunch, asking him to get as much detail about James Keeney's most recent incarceration, and the death of Sarah Mathews Bridgeton. We started walking the long hall to Haithem's office. I still couldn't call it my office. I knew he'd be back, but for now, it was better if people believed he was dead. At least, that's what he and Patrick Murphy, my – shit, I don't even know what to call him – believed.

We walked past Dalton's desk and entered the expansive, well-appointed office. Haithem had impeccable taste in everything. A large, brown, leather sofa sat against one wall. In front of it was a hand-carved, ornately detailed wood table. He'd gotten it from Morocco if memory served. In front of his desk, were two high-backed, brown leather chairs. He wasn't much of a collector, but he did have two beautiful paintings on the wall behind his desk. In all the years we'd known each other, I'd never asked him about them, but after spending the past few months in his position, I wanted to know the story behind them. There was always a story behind the items he chose to display.

"Ms. Jackson, here are the records for Mr. Keeney. It appears that his recent incarceration is the result of habitual B&Es." I knew that already, but I let Dalton continue. "He's serving ten years for his most recent offense."

"And what about Bridgeton?"

"Now that is interesting." He handed me a second file. "Sarah Mathews Bridgeton is the daughter of Michael Allen Mathews, the famed investor."

I shrugged and shook my head.

"You don't know who he is?"

"Not a clue."

Dalton proceeded to give me every detail about Michael Allen Mathews. The guy was married for more than fifty years. They had three children—Sarah and Michelle, who were twins, and Michael Allen, Jr. Michael Allen, Sr. was worth millions. The estate was split among the kids when he and his wife died.

According to several articles Dalton had found, the couple's private jet had crashed into the side of a mountain three years ago.

"Well, that sucks. I was kind of hoping for a happier ending. Where are the siblings?"

"Michael Mathews lives in Omaha, but Michelle is a wanderer. Her last known address was in New York City, but that was several years ago."

"What about Sarah Mathew's husband? What's his name?"

"Cal Bridgeton. He's still the Chief Executive Officer for Bridgeton and Myers. His partner is Sam Myers. He's the Chief Financial Officer."

"What kind of firm is it?"

"A prominent engineering company, but they're pretty leveraged from what I could dig up so far."

"I'll start with them. See if you can get me a meeting with Bridgeton."

FRIDAY MORNING, I PULLED my Jeep into the parking lot of Bridgeton & Myers. The building extended at least ten stories into an overcast sky. When I'd left my house, it smelled as if it was going to rain, not one of those cool, cleansing rains, but more like a torrential downpour, so I'd grabbed my raincoat and an umbrella. I opened my Jeep door; rain began pounding the ground, and me right with it. I slammed my car door, headed for the entrance to the building, and nearly ran a guy down in the process.

"Oh, wow! I'm so sorry," I said, as he fumbled with the door and opened it so I could pass in front of him.

"Not at all! Please, after you."

He followed me inside and we took a minute to shake off the extra water.

"May I help you find someone?"

"Yes, thank you. I'm here to see Cal Bridgeton."

He smiled.

"You're Cal Bridgeton?"

He nodded.

"Hi, I'm Dezeray Jackson." I wiped my hand on my pant leg, and then extended it to him.

"It's a pleasure to meet you, Ms. Jackson. Why don't we go upstairs to my office and get a cup of coffee to warm up?"

"That would be great."

We rode the elevator in uncomfortable silence to the tenth floor. When the doors opened, he motioned for me to precede him. A small reception area occupied by a woman, two men, and the receptionist, who according to the nameplate on his desk, was Daniel, all looked in our direction. Cal Bridgeton acknowledged the guests with a nod and simple hello.

"Daniel, this is Ms. Jackson. She's early for our appointment, so please let the others know that I'll be with them shortly."

By others, I assumed he meant the people waiting in the reception area, but I wasn't sure. Clearly, they had just heard what he said to Daniel.

"Shall we get that cup of coffee?"

I followed him into a large office. To the left of the door there was a seating area. To the right, his desk. An expansive bookshelf lined the wall behind his desk and was filled with engineering and business books. After taking my coat, he invited me to sit on the couch. A moment later, Daniel entered the room with a tray holding two cups of coffee, creamer, and sugar. He set it onto a table between us.

"Thank you, Daniel."

Daniel smiled. Not a genuine smile. It was more like annoyance, with a side of scorn. I made a mental note to have a chat with him.

"So, Ms. Jackson, how may I help you?" Bridgeton sat across from me with a clear view of the door.

When Dalton made this appointment, he was careful not to reveal what my intentions were. I wasn't confident that Cal Bridgeton would want to help James Keeney prove his innocence.

"I'm looking into the death of your former spouse, Sarah."

He shifted in his seat, crossed his legs, and folded his hands in his lap.

"That's been resolved. What questions could you possibly have? The police notified me that they found her killer already in prison. Someone named James Keeney."

"Yes, they did, however, I've been retained by Mr. Keeney."

"Retained by Keeney? Why?"

"He says he didn't kill your wife and he found her, alive, when he broke into your Regency home."

Another shift. Either his chair was very uncomfortable, or I'd hit a nerve.

"The police assured me that Keeney killed my wife. They found DNA belonging to him in my house."

"That's true, but from what I understand, there's nothing connecting him to stabbing your wife."

"You're here to help him get away with it."

"No. I'm here trying to decide whether the police have the right person. Keeney has a long history of breaking and entering, but not of violence. His record is clean on that front. It doesn't make sense that he'd change his MO and stab someone."

"It does if she surprised him, which is what the police believe happened."

"Look, I understand your need for closure, more than you know, but what if he isn't the person who killed your wife? That would mean the killer is still out there, and an innocent man is likely going to spend the rest of his life in prison."

Bridgeton stood and walked to his desk. Without turning back, he said, "He's not innocent."

The meeting was over, as far as Bridgeton was concerned.

"Mr. Bridgeton," I said, as I set my coffee on the table and stood to leave. "If you could just tell me what happened that night, the things you remember, I'd appreciate it."

When he turned to face me, creases had formed across his forehead and his jaw had tightened.

"Everything you need to know is in the police reports."

"Mr. Bridgeton?"

"We're finished here."

I thanked him for his time, grabbed my coat from a rack by the door, and left his office, closing the door behind me. More people were waiting in the reception area, and Daniel was sitting at his desk clicking at his computer keyboard.

"Daniel?"

He looked up and smiled. "Yes, Ms. Jackson?"

"Have you worked here long?"

"Since the beginning."

"About seven years, then?"

"Uh, huh."

"So, you probably knew Mrs. Bridgeton?"

"Oh, yes. Lovely woman. Fabulous sense of style. It's too bad what happened to her."

"I'd love to talk with you more about that sometime."

He sat up straighter, and leaned forward as if he had some secret to share.

"I could tell you so much more."

"Really, like what?"

Cal Bridgeton's office door opened. Startled, Daniel sat back and pretended to look for something, then he scribbled his contact information onto a small piece of paper. Handing it to me, he said, "Ms. Jackson, these are the directions you need. It shouldn't take you more than a few minutes to get there from here."

"Daniel, please send in the first applicant," Bridgeton said. "Ms. Jackson, if there's nothing else, we have work to do."

"Thanks, Daniel," I said.

I waited until the elevator doors closed, and then read the note. Daniel wanted to meet for lunch at a place called Flare. It was new. I hadn't been there but read about it in the *Omaha World-Herald*. Flare opened a few months ago with a menu designed to test your spice limits. The chef, the article said, was influenced and inspired by Thai, Indian, and Spanish cuisine to create an infusion of taste sensations. When I read that, I knew I had to try it.

Daniel and I wouldn't be meeting for a few hours, so I took a quick trip to the library on Ninetieth and Dodge Streets to do some research. The crime-scene files weren't accessible, but I could read all the articles the paper wrote at the time. I was pretty sure I'd also find a video or two. Someone like Sarah Mathews-Bridgeton doesn't get killed without a whole lot of news media coverage.

After an hour of searching through the online database of the *Omaha World-Herald*, and reading at least fifteen articles about Sarah Bridgeton's murder, I felt good about my understanding of what the police, and public, believed happened. Cal Bridgeton had been attending a late meeting with a potential client. When he returned home, he discovered Sarah's body in their living room and called the police. One article reported there was a delay between the time he found her and when he called the police, but no other articles followed up about the discrepancy. The police spent months investigating Cal Bridgeton, but never found anything connecting him to his wife's death. They had to rule it a homicide, and it ended up in the Cold-case Unit.

I decided I needed more information about the Bridgetons, so I began searching past issues of *Omaha Magazine*, *The Reader*, *Encounter*, and *Omaha Home*. Several articles about Sarah's charity work appeared in *Omaha Magazine* and *The Reader*, and one profile about her family, before she married Cal Bridgeton, appeared in *Encounter*. She and her sister weren't just twins, they were identical. Their younger brother, by two years, resembled them so much that he could have been a fraternal sibling. They'd all attended Brownell-Talbot. The twins graduated from Creighton University. Michael studied business before joining his father's company after graduating. Sarah earned an economics degree and eventually began working for various nonprofit groups.

Michelle was the maverick. She skipped graduation, opting to travel instead. Eventually, she landed jobs in the fashion industry, usually, as an assistant. At the time of the article, Michelle was living in New York City.

My search continued and I found articles announcing Sarah and Cal's wedding. Their ceremony was at the Joslyn Castle about five years ago. By all accounts, Cal and Sarah Bridgeton were a happy couple and involved in the community. They knew or had access to all the right people, mostly because of Sarah's parents. That was probably what eventually led to the police stopping their investigation of Cal Bridgeton. Being connected to powerful people, alive or dead, could keep you out of trouble. That, and nothing useful at the crime scene.

Their marriage happened two years after Bridgeton and Sam Myers started their firm. Now, Bridgeton & Myers is one of the top engineering companies in Omaha, NE. How the hell does that happen in such a short time?

Whoever killed Sarah Bridgeton was meticulous, and that wasn't James Keeney's MO. The guy was always getting caught. It's how I gave him a beat-down in the first place. No, meticulousness wasn't Keeney's strength. The police found his DNA near a phone that had been knocked to the ground, presumably, during a struggle. A vibration from my phone on the table showed that I'd received a notification. It was a reminder to meet Daniel, so I closed out of the system and headed to Flare.

FLARE WAS IN A STRIP mall at 103rd and Pacific Streets. I entered the parking lot nearest to Trader Joe's and wound around until I got to the other side, closer to Pacific Street, and parked. I saw Daniel smoking a cigarette outside the restaurant and decided to wait for him to finish. After I saw him go inside, I got out of my Jeep and followed him.

The entrance of Flare was adorned with a series of fabric flames reaching to the ceiling. Coordinated lighting and a hidden blower made the effect eye-catching. The hostess greeted me, but I'd already located Daniel and walked past her to join him. He'd selected a table near the windows facing the parking lot. I slid into the booth across from him and saw that he was enjoying a Cosmo. Two waters, a basket of sliced bread, and a small saucer of herb-infused oil rested on the table.

"I thought you'd like water. I mean, who doesn't like water, right?"

"Thanks."

A server arrived tableside to give us a few recommendations. To keep things simple, I ordered a chicken dish that she'd suggested, and that I couldn't pronounce, and was assured it was amazing. Daniel did the same. I stuck with water while he ordered a second Cosmo.

"Daniel, I get the impression that you're not too fond of working for Cal Bridgeton."

He sipped his drink, hiding a partial grin, then set his glass onto the table, and said, "You're very astute."

"Well, it's in the job description."

The server returned with Daniel's drink. He downed the first and handed the empty glass to her.

"Why keep working for him?"

He sighed, and then said, "It's the money, honey. Cal Bridgeton pays well. There aren't many assistant positions that would pay me what he does. But he is an asshole. There's no way around that."

"What about Sam Myers?"

"Sam? Oh, he's a big doll. Wouldn't hurt anyone. He's another reason I stay."

"I read that they met during college."

"Yep. They were frat buddies. Hard to believe Sam would get involved in that sort of thing, but I guess he was what they call a legacy. Anyhoo, they came together a few years after college, and the rest, as they say, is history."

"What about Bridgeton and Sarah? What can you tell me about their relationship?"

He took another sip of his Cosmo before answering. "Well, they were just like a fairy tale, except that Cal isn't exactly Prince Charming."

"What do you mean?"

"That man couldn't keep it in his pants if someone told him it was going to fall off."

"Really? By all accounts, they were a happy couple."

"Oh, they were. I mean Sarah, God rest her soul, had no clue what he was up to, or rather, with whom, and he was content with the arrangement for a while. But then her father got involved."

"How so?"

"About a year before Mr. and Mrs. Mathews were killed, Mr. Mathews showed up at the firm unannounced and walked right into Mr. Bridgeton's office. Mr. Bridgeton had a special guest." He put air quotes around special.

"Where were you?"

"I had just stepped out for a cigarette break. Mr. Bridgeton was livid when I returned, but in the end, he forgave me."

"Who was in his office?"

"No one important. I mean I can't even recall her name."

"Did he see her regularly?"

"No, not this one. She was strictly a one-time thing."

"But there were others?"

"Oh, honey, there were several, with a capital "S", but not after Mr. Mathews' unannounced visit. At least, not for a longtime.

"But he started seeing other women again, at some point?"

"Yes, about a year before Mrs. Bridgeton was killed, I know he was seeing someone, but I don't know who she was, or if he's still seeing her."

"What makes you think he started seeing someone, again?"

"I found panties stuck between the cushions of the couch in his office."

AFTER MY ENLIGHTENING lunch with Daniel, I returned home to check on Godfrey, my Rottweiler. He'd been acting a little strange lately—not eating his usual small bag of dog food with a pizza chaser. When I unlocked the door to my house, I couldn't hear him on the other side. I tossed my leather satchel onto a chair as I walked through the living room to the kitchen. It was too quiet. Nothing seemed out of place, until I entered the kitchen and saw Godfrey laying on his bed, panting. He'd thrown up near the back door. When I walked to him and patted his head, he growled.

"Okay, Godfrey. It looks like you need to see the doctor." He closed his eyes. I wasn't sure how I was going to get him into the car. The damn dog weighed a ton and was longer than I am tall.

After cleaning up the floor, I found the number for my vet. When he told me that he could come out to see Godfrey, I knew it wasn't going to be a cheap visit, but I didn't have any other choice. I made sure Godfrey had a full dish of water and offered him his favorite treat - a piece of steak, but he didn't move. An hour later, my doorbell rang.

"Thanks for coming, Dr. Roberts."

He followed me into the kitchen. I watched helplessly, like a nervous mother seeing her kid get a shot, as he got on the floor to examine Godfrey.

"Did you keep the vomit?"

Um, no. Why would anyone keep dog vomit? He interrupted my thoughts and asked again.

"It's in the trash can. I used a bunch of paper towels."

He got up, located the can next to the back door, and grabbed the towels.

"Do you have a Ziplock bag?" he asked.

I'd already gotten one from the drawer next to the fridge. One thing about dog puke is that, fortunately, it doesn't fill the room like cat vomit does.

"I'm going to have to run a few tests to see if I can determine what's wrong. He's lethargic, but I didn't see any obvious injuries. For now, just let him rest, make sure he has plenty of water, and offer him food. He probably won't eat it but offer it anyway."

"How long before you'll know something?"

He checked his watch. "Probably not until morning. My best guess right now is that he simply ate something that didn't agree with him. I could take him back to the clinic with me, if that will make you feel better."

I swear I heard the *ching ching* of a cash register.

"Honestly, maybe that would be a good idea." I got Godfrey's leash from a hook by the back door, and this time he didn't growl at me when I attached it to his collar. "Come on, Godfrey. You need to go with Dr. Roberts." Godfrey tried to raise himself, then fell back to the floor. I looked at Dr. Roberts, panicked.

"Here, let me." He scooped Godfrey up. "Can you grab my bag?"

I walked ahead of him to open the doors. Outside, he placed Godfrey on the front passenger seat of his pickup.

"Try not to worry. I'll call you if there are any more issues." He hopped into his truck, and I watched as he drove away.

Godfrey has an iron stomach. That dog eats anything, so I was finding it hard to believe something didn't agree with him, but Dr. Roberts was a good vet. If he wasn't too worried, then I shouldn't be. When I returned to the house, I could hear the phone in my office ringing. I ran to answer it, but it stopped just before I snatched it up. After a few minutes, the tiny red message light blinked. I tapped in my security code, listened to a few prompts, and heard the message. Patrick Murphy wanted to meet.

ON THE WAY OUT THE door to meet Murphy at Eddy's Billiard Hall, I grabbed my cue. True, this was a business meeting, but it was Friday night, and I could probably pick up a couple hundred pretty easily.

When I arrived at Eddy's, I waved to Mack from across the road. He was one of the bouncers. Mack wasn't his name, but it suited him. He opened the door and the familiar aroma of burgers and fries wafted out. I hadn't had dinner and didn't know what I wanted until this moment.

"Busy night?" I asked, before letting the door close behind me.

"It's gettin there, Ms. D. You plannin on schooling a few young bloods this evening?"

I smiled and continued inside. Scanning the room, I saw that several tables were occupied by college kids, probably from the University of Nebraska-Omaha. Sometimes, I'd find a kid who knew his way around the table but couldn't quite finish the game. Tonight, didn't look like one of those kinds of nights.

Murphy was seated at the far end of the bar talking with Eddy. It'd been a month since we'd last seen each other. Our phone calls were always brief, and we avoided e-mail, so I was eager to catch up. The fact he'd decided we needed to meet, meant something had changed. I leaned my stick against the counter and took the stool next to his.

"The usual?" Eddy asked.

"Yeah, thanks."

"You're looking good, love," Murphy said, and kissed my cheek.

"What's going on?"

"Ready to jump right in, eh?"

"It's been a month, Murphy. Has Haithem figured anything else out about Scott and the Alec Covington issue?"

Eddy returned with my gin and tonic.

"You going to eat?" Eddy asked us.

I ordered a cheeseburger with bacon, fries, and onion rings, 'cause my arteries were feeling up to the challenge. Murphy just ordered two cheeseburgers.

"I'm not sharing my fries and rings," I said.

"Yeah, ya are. You know you can't eat all that."

"No bunny food, then?" Eddy asked.

"Maybe next time," I said, smiling.

"To answer your question," Murphy turned his stool toward me. "Haithem found more details about Abaci Transportation Corporation and a possible connection to a senator."

"Which senator?"

"He's still checking things out, so I can't give you that just yet."

"What about Scott?"

"Nearest we can tell, he went off grid and whoever is left of his group hasn't surfaced, either." He finished his beer, and signaled Eddy for another round.

"What about the knife? Was The Lab able to find anything?"

"No, not yet. They have some new tech that might help, but I don't know the ins and outs of it. I'm in a holding pattern."

"Have you told your dad about any of this, yet?"

"No."

"Are you going to?"

"Not, yet. There's no point. All I know is that whoever killed Savannah sure as hell wasn't some homeless guy. He had skills more like..."

"Me."

"Yeah, a lot like you. And I don't know whether Scott or Covington, or even this possible senator have anything to do with Savannah's murder." I stopped for a minute to take that in. This was the first time I'd used that word about my sister out loud. I reached for my drink and noticed that my hand trembled. I'd been compartmentalizing everything since learning about Scott's connection to Savannah. Every inch of me wanted to beat him into the ground for lying to me and using me to further his agenda.

Murphy rested his hand on my thigh and said, "Haithem is close. We'll have more information soon, and then we can move this thing forward."

I nodded my head and picked up my drink. Eddy returned with our food, saw my empty glass, and asked, "Refill?"

"I'll have a beer, instead. Thanks, Eddy."

"Anything else I need to know about?" Murphy asked. "Any strange packages lately?"

"No. Godfrey's sick."

"Seriously? What's wrong with him?"

"I don't know. The vet took him for the night. He wouldn't eat and couldn't get up."

"I'm happy to take his place tonight."

I shoved his shoulder and started eating my food, guarding my fries and rings from his grabby hands. He finally gave up and ordered a basket of fries.

CHAPTER TWO

MURPHY LEFT MY PLACE early so he could get back to wherever he was hiding Haithem, and I opted to stay in bed longer. Some people do the planning and organizing of their day in the shower; not me. I lie in bed, take a few deep breaths to clear my head, and start creating my schedule. Today, I needed to hit the gym to train. I hadn't had any decent training partners lately. Most of the regulars trained in the evening and that rarely worked for me. By the end of the day, I'm too damn exhausted or still trailing some dumbass cheating on their spouse. People like to assume it's the guys doing the most cheating, but from my experience it's about a fifty-fifty split in Omaha, NE.

After the gym, I needed to deliver the news about one of those situations. Two weeks ago, I was hired by a man to investigate his girlfriend. He planned to propose, but there were a series of recent incidents that made him question his decision. The woman was careful, but I got her. She's been hooking up with a guy in her office at a hotel in west Omaha. I hate giving people this kind of news, but at least he'll be able to walk away clean. They don't have any kids. He can get back to climbing the social and business ladders of Omaha. He'd already been featured in the *Midlands Business Journal's 40 Under 40 annual piece.*

I also needed to track down Michael Mathews. From Dalton's preliminary research, I knew that he was a backer for an upscale, trendy restaurant that opened near Thirty-eighth and Farnam in the Blackstone neighborhood. Whether I'd get lucky and find him there tonight wasn't a chance I wanted to take, so I'd have Dalton do the legwork and get back to me with confirmation of Mathews' location. Then there was the knife. That pleasant thought motivated me to get my ass out of bed.

The knife was a gift from Alec Covington, Scott James' crew. They'd left it in my house, wrapped. Godfrey found it, and being the smart dog that he is, only damaged it a little with his teeth when he picked it up and brought it to me. They wanted me to believe it was the murder weapon in Savannah's case, but I was beginning to think that was bullshit. A knife wasn't in the original crime-scene pictures, and I still didn't have a good explanation for that. The autopsy report listed her cause of death as the result of several stab wounds to the stomach and lower back, but something about that didn't feel right.

Savannah was a skilled fighter. Whoever murdered her had to have surprised her, but I couldn't believe she didn't struggle or resist. I was fifteen when we got the news that Savannah was killed. She was my best friend. A familiar, dull ache started in my trap muscle and slowly made its way up the right side of my neck and to the base of my skull. This happened every time I thought about my sister's case and that her killer hasn't been found. I rolled my head around, shrugged a few times, then punched the heavy bag hanging in the corner of my bedroom.

Since I planned to work out, I put on gi pants and a long-sleeve rash guard, gathered my curls into a braid, and went downstairs to the kitchen. It felt strange not seeing Godfrey in his bed, not that he spent much time there at night. Usually, he'd follow me upstairs and sleep at the end of my bed, or in the doorway leading back into the hall. Hopefully, Dr. Roberts would call soon and tell me what's wrong.

By the time I left the house, it was ten o'clock. I kept some of my training gear in the Jeep but had grabbed my sai on the way out. If no one else was available to train sai, I knew that Master Simmons would indulge me.

Simmons Martial Arts Academy was twenty minutes from my place and located in the Benson Business District. Training at Simmons reminded me of the years I'd spent training in my parents' dojang. The place wasn't big, but it always was busy.

When I arrived, a Little Dragons class was in session. The little kids all stood inside small hula hoops, practicing their front kicks, blocks, and punches. After they finished, each child sat inside their designated spaces and awaited further instructions. Master Simmons smiled and gave me a little nod as I walked behind the students and crossed the mat.

"Sai, huh? It's been one of those kinds of mornings, has it?"

"Lots on my mind."

"All right, then. Let's get to it." I followed him into the rear training room. "You know, you're the only student I've ever had who took to this weapon immediately. I remember when you first tried them."

"Me, too. I still have the scar."

After thirty minutes getting my ass handed to me, we stopped. Master Simmons guided me through a bag workout, and we ended with grappling. I'm still waiting for the day when I can take him down and keep him there.

"You're still pretty spry for an old guy." I tossed a handbag at him.

"Old guy, huh? You know I'm only sixty-seven."

"Yeah," I said, stifling a laugh.

"Well, clearly, I can still keep up with you."

After the session with Master Simmons, I got cleaned up. One of the great things about this dojang is that he built locker rooms in the basement. Not many dojangs have them, and believe me, it's nice to get other people's sweaty nastiness off you as soon as possible after training.

From Simmons, I decided to grab some lunch. On the way to Zio's on Dodge Street, my phone rang so I pulled into a parking lot to take the call. Dalton found information about Michael Mathews' evening plans. I didn't bother asking him how. Sometimes it's better not to know everything Dalton does. Plausible deniability. Attending a fund-raising gala this evening became my top priority.

THE GALA WAS IN A WAREHOUSE-turned-art studio in the Old Market district. Parking downtown sucked, especially on a weekend. I couldn't find a spot anywhere on the street when I arrived and had to wait fifteen minutes before one opened in a lot a block away from the event. Walking that block in heels was enough to sour my mood by the time I reached the entrance. I was wearing my favorite little black dress, though. It had a hidden compartment sewn into the hemline where I could stash a mini-recording device, cash, and a credit-card size, thin metal multitool. The multitool is a woman's best friend and I own several.

Sparkling lights decorated the entrance, and a greeter opened the door, ushering me inside. A tunnel of balloons led guests into an open space filled with round, high tables covered in black linens. There weren't any chairs, but several cushioned benches lined the perimeter. A stage had been placed near the back of the room. A band played smooth jazz while people mingled and ate tiny appetizers from trays held by staff members dressed as mimes. I scanned the room for Michael Mathews. A mime passed me with a tray of champagne, and I grabbed one so that I'd blend in better.

After an hour, I'd still not seen Mathews and began to wonder whether Dalton's information was correct. I laughed at the thought. Dalton's information was always correct; I needed to wait it out a little longer. Then I saw Mathews near the stage talking with two women. One had short-cropped hair styled in a pixie cut. The other woman's hair was long and an unnatural shade of red. I walked in their direction, but stopped as the women took the stage.

"We'd like to thank all of you for coming out to support the arts this evening," the woman with the pixie cut said. "Your generous gifts will allow us to continue to provide free art classes to our area youth who are disadvantaged."

"And because you've all been so kind, we'd like to announce our new program designed to allow those same children an opportunity to travel to France this year, where they'll be able to visit not only Notre Dame, but also the Louvre," the redhead said.

The crowd applauded their own kindness and generosity. The women continued talking, but I tuned them out to keep an eye on Mathews, who by now had moved toward the front of the space. He was alone, which from what I knew of him, wasn't a common occurrence. I approached him while another mime wandered between us with an appetizer tray. As he reached for one, I did the same, causing us to touch fingers. This led to a few "excuse mes," but gave me the opening I wanted. The mime had scurried away, leaving us without appetizers.

"Aren't you Michael Mathews?" I asked.

"Yes, and who do I have the pleasure of meeting this evening?"

"Dezeray. Dezeray Jackson."

"A beautiful name for a beautiful woman." He smiled and extended his hand. "Are you enjoying the gala?"

"Yes, it's lovely." My inner hoity-toity came out in full force. "And you?"

"These events are always entertaining, but I'm really just here for the free appetizers and champagne." We laughed at that. "Seriously, though, I do enjoy supporting this particular art center's programs. They seem genuinely passionate about helping children through art." He sipped his champagne. "How about you?"

"I'm a freelance writer and I thought this might be a good event to cover. My focus is the arts."

"I can introduce you to the organizers, if you'd like?"

"That would be wonderful, but I'd also love to hear more about you and what motivates you to donate to these types of programs."

He checked his Rolex. "Would you care to join me for a drink and dessert at my restaurant?"

"You have a restaurant? I thought your family was strictly into bigger investments."

"It's a side project. Something different, and honestly, it's fun. Shall we?" He gestured toward the door. "It's not far from here. Just west in the Blackstone neighborhood."

"I'll meet you there. I don't want to leave my car here."

"I understand. I'll see you there in a few minutes."

"That sounds great! I'll just finish up a few conversations here before I go."

We parted and I pretended to mingle with a few attendees, gathering information for the article that I'd never write, just in case he was still watching me.

VIBE WAS IN AN OLD strip of buildings at Thirty-eighth and Farnam Streets, about five minutes from downtown. The adjoining parking lot was full, so I found a spot a block west. I checked the time; It was 9:30 p.m. People streamed in and out of the area bars. The crowds in this part of town skewed older than college age, but generally younger than sixty.

The entryway was wall-to-wall with people waiting for a table. I snaked my way through the crowd to the host stand. She directed me to the bar, which was separated from the main dining area by a brick wall that didn't reach the exposed ceilings. The acoustics were horrible. I wasn't sure how anyone could have a conversation in this place. I saw Mathews sitting at a table near the far end of the bar and joined him. He stood to greet me and pulled out my chair. That was new.

"I took the liberty of ordering a bottle of wine and a small cheese plate. I hope that's okay."

"That sounds great."

A server appeared tableside with a bottle of Decero Malbec Remolinos Vineyard Agrelo, a plate of sliced Manchego, and a bowl of roasted cashews. My stomach rumbled. I hadn't eaten much of the appetizers at the gala and now I was starving.

"Antonio makes the most amazing chocolate-caramel flan you'll ever find. Shall I order that, too?"

"Oh, my God, yes, please do," I said and took a slice of cheese as he poured the wine. "How long has Vibe been open?"

"Only a few months."

"Is it usually this packed?"

"It's been well-received. We're only open Wednesday through Saturday, with a limited in-season menu. This allows Antonio to be his most creative self. Much of what he serves is influenced by his Argentinian roots, but he does enjoy experimenting."

"How did you get involved in the restaurant?"

"Antonio and I met during a month-long trip I took to Buenos Aires last year. He had a restaurant there and I was a frequent visitor during my stay. When he mentioned wanting to come to the United States to open a restaurant, I offered to help."

"Buenos Aires? What took you there?"

"I was visiting my sister, Michelle."

"Oh, I'd forgotten that you had a sister. Is that where she lives?"

"No, she's somewhat nomadic. It was just another place for her to explore."

"Nomadic tendencies must be a family trait, since you left work for a month to join her."

"Maybe a little. But enough about me. What about you? Why freelance writing?"

"I love having my freedom."

"But it must come with a lot of uncertainty."

"Maybe a little." I smiled and took a handful of cashews from the bowl.

"What makes a multimillionaire investor decide to support art classes for poor kids?"

"It's something my sister started, and I wanted to keep doing it, after her..." He sipped his wine. "I don't know how much you already know about my family."

"Not much, really."

"I have—had two sisters. Sarah was killed a few years ago. Michelle is her identical twin. She's been having a few challenges since Sarah's death."

"Oh, I'm so sorry to have brought this all up." I reached out and touched his hand. I find that I can get people to share more when I do this, and Michael wasn't any different than anyone else. The sign on my forehead read: Tell me anything. In short order, he unloaded details about Sarah's death—most of which I had already discovered—but then, one surprising thing was revealed.

"It sounds like you don't care much for Cal Bridgeton."

"No, I don't. My parents didn't, either. Initially, when they met, he seemed nice enough. And he was building a successful engineering firm. Then something changed."

"What?"

As if he suddenly realized he'd been saying too much, he leaned back and sat straighter in his chair. This interview was over. For now.

The server returned to check on us and Michael ordered the chocolate-caramel flan. "Would you like more wine?" I nodded, and he poured. "Are you from Omaha?"

"Yes, originally, but then my family moved often. My father was in the military." When constructing a lie, it's always easier if you keep things as close to the truth as possible. I usually only change my career and omit a few finer details about my family.

"Any siblings?" he asked, as he retrieved cheese from the plate between us.

"Three. All older."

"Ah, so you're the baby, too." He laughed a little at that. He was becoming comfortable, again. "Mine were always putting me in dresses when we were young, but you probably didn't have that experience."

"No, can't say that I did, but I have brothers and one sister."

"Is your family in Omaha, now?"

"No, they're spread out. I returned because my Great Aunt Violet left me her house. Passing up a free house didn't seem prudent, given my career path."

"Beautiful and sensible."

I felt my cheeks get hot and was thankful that in this dimly lit space he couldn't see it.

"I'm surprised that someone like you hasn't gotten snatched up." The man was eye candy. His dark, short, wavy hair accented his blue eyes. When he smiled, one dimple showed in his left cheek. His six-foot frame was lean beneath his brown, pinstripe jacket and slacks. Definitely doable. Dateable, maybe, but doable, hell, yes.

The server brought our flan on a single plate with two forks. We each took small bites. The creaminess of the flan lingered on my tongue. He split the rest of the wine between our two glasses. The combination of the flan and the wine created a smooth, full sensation. I closed my eyes, concentrating on the pleasure of the layered tastes.

"I could order another bottle."

My eyes popped open. "As much as I would love that, I still need to get home."

"Another time, then?"

"I'd like that."

"Good. I don't think I've given you what you need for your article, yet."

We exchanged contact information.

"Perhaps we could get together for brunch tomorrow?"

"I have plans tomorrow. How about lunch later this week? I'll call you."

"It's a date."

"Well, not yet." I smiled and stood to leave.

"I'll walk you to your car."

"No, that's okay, I'm fine."

"Dez, it's late, and as much as I like this neighborhood, there are some bad elements at this hour. Let me walk you. It'll make me feel better."

We walked in relaxed silence to my Jeep. After I unlocked it, he opened the door for me, then reaching for my hand, and kissed it. I didn't think men did that anymore. Taken aback, I climbed onto the seat and said goodnight. He shut the door, and I could see in my rear-view mirror that he'd moved to the sidewalk and was watching me drive away.

MONDAY MORNING, I CALLED Daniel at Bridgeton & Myers to see whether he could meet me for lunch. He didn't seem like the kind of guy who'd pass up an opportunity for someone else to pay his way, or to gossip. He didn't prove me wrong. This time, I suggested we meet at Zio's Pizzeria on Dodge. He was as excited about my restaurant choice as someone hearing that they need a root canal, but I wasn't about to lay down another sixty bucks for lunch. He could eat pizza and have a beer.

After I made arrangements to meet Daniel for lunch, I called in to my Lincoln office to let Dalton know my plans for the day, and to get him searching for Michelle Mathews. I wasn't sure how I was going to approach her, if we found her, but I felt as if I needed to learn more about what she was up to.

I arrived at Zio's before Daniel. We'd planned to meet at 12:30 p.m., but he sent me a text saying he was running behind because of a meeting. I ordered a beer and caught up on email while I waited for him. The lunch crowd had diminished as people rushed to return to their jobs. Just after one o'clock, I saw Daniel get out of his car and walk to the entrance. I waved to him as he entered.

"I haven't been here in ages," he said, sliding into the booth opposite mine.

"Welcome back. You've missed some great pizza."

The server came over, gave Daniel a water, took our order, and then sauntered away to give it to the kitchen. Her sense of urgency clearly much lower than a mere fifteen minutes ago.

"I met Michael Mathews this past weekend."

"Really? Isn't he handsome?" Daniel fiddled with his straw wrapper. "I met him a few times, and oi, what I'd give to look like him."

There wasn't anything extraordinary about Daniel's appearance except his clothes. He didn't shy away from color, and he seemed to have a knack for combining patterns you normally wouldn't think could work together.

"Did you ever meet his sister, Michelle?"

"As a matter of fact, she was in the office frequently for a while there, a few years ago."

"Why?"

"She and Mr. Myers had a thing."

"A thing?"

"Yes."

"Are you sure?"

He shook his head.

"So, Bridgeton married Sarah and Myers had a thing for her sister?"

"It didn't last long. Maybe a few months. She just stopped showing up."

"How long ago was that?"

He peered out the window for a minute before answering. "I want to say that it was maybe a few months after they started seeing each other. It was a whirlwind romance."

"How did Bridgeton react to their romance?"

"Now that you mention it, he seemed miffed."

"Jealous?"

He nodded. "I never understood why Mr. Myers decided to partner with Bridgeton."

"Why's that?"

"Bridgeton is a competitive man. With everyone and everything, including Mr. Myers."

"Why do you think Bridgeton was jealous of Mr. Myers? Bridgeton was already married to Sarah."

"But he's the kind of guy who wants all the attention, from everyone, all the time. He thinks he's E.F. Hutton."

I let that sink in a minute, partly because I couldn't believe Daniel knew about E.F. Hutton.

"After Myers split from Michelle, what did Bridgeton do?"

"By then, he'd moved on to another woman?"

"Do you know who?"

"No, I never saw her."

"MS. JACKSON? THIS IS Dalton. I located Ms. Mathews and she's no longer out of the country."

I checked the time; it was six o'clock in the morning. Right about now, I wanted to reach through the phone and strangle Dalton.

"Where is she?"

"New Orleans. She's staying in the Garden District with a friend."

"What kind of friend?"

"Male. Mid-forties. He owns a nightclub in the French Quarter."

"God, doesn't every forty-something male in New Orleans' Garden District?"

"I don't have that information, Ms. Jackson."

"Dalton, I was being sarcastic. Thanks for the info. I'll let you know whether I need anything else. And Dalton?"

"Yes, Ms. Jackson?"

"Don't call me this early unless someone's seriously hurt, and I give a shit in some way, or someone is dead, and I know them."

"Yes, Ms. Jackson."

The line cut off and I set my phone back on the nightstand. As much as I would have loved to roll over and go back to sleep, that wasn't going to happen. Once I'm up, I'm up. Not stumbling over Godfrey still wasn't something I was used to. Dr. Roberts left a message Monday afternoon letting me know that he was waiting for test results. He said Godfrey was resting, but because he wasn't eating, they inserted a tube into his digestive tract. I knew Godfrey was a tough dog, but this was the first time he'd been this ill. In the past when he'd throw up, it was because he ate too much pizza.

I rolled out of bed, showered, and dressed in fifteen minutes. Breakfast was a fried-egg sandwich with cheese like I used to have when I lived in New York City. I never made it myself, there; I'd get it from the diner at the corner of my block. Sometimes I missed New York; other times I was thankful I left.

Now that I knew where Michelle was, I also knew who to call to help me get a bead on her – Charlie "Bobo" LaRoche. He was my partner back in Miami. Before I left for New York City, he had moved to New Orleans. Like me, he'd opted to go out on his own. I scrolled through the contacts on my phone and dialed his number.

"Speak to me," he said.

"Charlie Bobo LaRoche, it's been a minute. This is Dez Jackson."

"Dez! How you been, girl? I heard you returned to Nebraska."

"Yep. A free house is hard to pass up."

"True enough."

"Listen, Charlie, I was wondering if you could do me a favor?"

"What kind of favor?"

"I need you to check someone out for me. Just basic stuff. Follow her. See who she's hangin with. That sort of thing."

"Who's this she?"

"Michelle Mathews. She's the daughter of a dead investment big shot named Michael Mathews."

"You got an address?"

I gave him her Garden District location.

"How long do you want me to watch her?"

"Hard to say. I'm trying to see what her connection might be to a few men here in Omaha."

"All right. I'll see what I can do. I got another case I'm workin. Strange lady, but she pays well."

"Strange lady in New Orleans? That's a surprise."

"You know I'm not into all that mystical, voodoo mumbo-jumbo shit, but this lady's been on point every step of the way. She's got me lookin for some dude named Cyrano Beautemps."

"Only in New Orleans, I swear. Where else would you ever find anyone naming their kid Cyrano?"

"You got that right. You got a picture of Mathews?"

"Yeah, I'll text it to you."

"Sounds good"

"I'll be in touch."

With that task completed, I decided to track down Sam Myers. Daniel mentioned that Myers liked to visit a local coffee shop every morning before arriving at the office around nine thirty. Rush Coffee is in the historic Dundee neighborhood north of Dodge Street.

THE AROMA OF FRESH-ground coffee, combined with the smell of sweet syrups, filled the air when I walked into Rush. Several customers waited in line to order while others eagerly anticipated that first sip. I spotted Sam Myers at a table in a corner near the back of the small shop. He was reading the *Omaha World-Herald,* intermittently taking sips from his coffee cup, and small bites of a large, chocolate muffin. I could play this two ways. Lie and slowly get information from him about Cal Bridgeton, or tell the truth and hope he'd go along with me. I'm a big fan of lying as long as I'm the one doing it, but I decided to roll the dice and tell the truth.

"Mr. Myers?"

He folded the paper and looked up at me.

"I'm Dezeray Jackson. And I'm..."

"Cal told me who you are." He set the paper to the side.

"Do you mind if I ask you a few questions?"

He gestured to the chair across from him. Sam Myers was a short man. Probably about five seven, or five eight, at the most. His head was bald, cheeks full, and he wore dark-rimmed glasses. He was good-looking in an off-the-wall way. Kind of like a pug.

"I'm not sure how I can help you with James Keeney's case. I was with Cal at the meeting that brought him home late the night Sarah was killed."

"How would you describe Mr. Bridgeton's relationship with his wife?"

He removed his glasses and began cleaning them with a napkin.

"Ms. Jackson, as far as I know, they were happy." He put his glasses back on and adjusted them.

"You two are close, so you must have known that he was cheating on Sarah."

"Of course, but that doesn't mean that he wasn't happy with her."

"Did you know the women he cheated with?"

"No, not really. I tried to stay out of that part of his life."

"I understand that you were seeing her sister, Michelle?"

He nodded. "Yes, briefly. We parted company on amicable terms. The relationship had run its course."

"Do you know who she was seeing after your split?"

"No. Honestly, I wasn't interested in knowing."

"Why do you think Bridgeton was jealous of your relationship with Michelle?"

"Who said that he was?"

"Someone mentioned it to me."

"Ah," he said, smiling. "The ever-present, ever-watchful Daniel?"

I didn't confirm it, but I also didn't deny it.

"I think Cal wants what he can't have until he actually has it."

"Did he have Michelle?"

"I really don't know."

"If he did have a relationship with Michelle, how would Michelle have reacted to his ending it?"

"You haven't had the pleasure of meeting her, have you?"

I shook my head.

"Michelle and Sarah were physically alike, but their personalities were drastically different. Let's just say that I got the crazy sister and leave it at that."

"When did Michelle leave Omaha?"

"It was probably a few months after we split. I'm not sure where she went."

My phone rang and I saw that it was Dr. Roberts. I thanked Myers for his time and left the coffee shop to return the call. No one answered so I waited a few minutes and tried again.

"Dr. Roberts' office," a woman answered.

I told her who I was and that I was returning his call. She put me on hold. After what seemed like forever, Dr. Roberts came on the line.

"Dez, things aren't looking good for Godfrey right now."

"Why? What happened?"

"He was poisoned. It looks like Godfrey got hold of some ibuprofen."

"I don't have any ibuprofen. I ran out of it a week ago."

"Well, somehow he ingested a fairly large amount. There were traces of meat in the bile sample, along with the drug. It's possible that he got into a neighbor's trash."

"No, he never gets out of the yard."

"We might never know exactly how it happened. For now, he's resting, but he's not out of the woods. We haven't been able to remove the tube. He's going to be here a little while longer."

I ended the call understanding that I was about to drop at least a grand on my dog because some asshole poisoned him. Don't get me wrong, I'm fine with paying the bill, but not knowing who did this to Godfrey was going to stay with me a longtime.

CHAPTER THREE

SINCE I HADN'T VISITED Keeney's girlfriend, Mazy, yet I thought I should check in with her and get my down payment. I'd already logged enough hours to warrant it. The drive took about twenty minutes; I found her place off Twenty-fourth and Vinton Streets. I parked on the street and walked the short path to the front door. Chipped white paint covered the exterior and the screened porch had bigger holes than a pair of fishnet stockings. The door slid slightly off its hinge and screeched as I opened it, and the floorboards creaked with each step I took toward the front door. I knocked. No one answered. I knocked again, but with more force. I heard someone on the inside stumble, and say, "Shit!" before opening the door.

"Are you Mazy?" I asked.

"Who wants to know?" She was short and pencil thin. Years of drinking and smoking had left their mark on her face.

"Keeney sent me. I'm Dezeray Jackson."

"Keeney sent you? That good for nothin son-of-a-bitch sent you here?"

Well, this wasn't what I expected.

"Yeah. He said you could pay me for my services. I'm investigating his current case."

"Current case. He's such a shit."

"You're probably right about that, but I'm supposed to collect payment from you."

Gesturing to the house and yard, she said, "Does it look like I got money for you? Really?"

"Look, he said you had his money. I'm just here to get my down payment."

"Sugar, I ain't got his money. That motherfucker got his ass pinched and I used all of it for his damn lawyer. A lot of good that done him."

"Keeney has a public defender."

"Yeah, now, but not before. That idiot has no clue."

"So, you're saying all of his money is gone?"

"That's what I'm telling you. Yeah."

God dammit.

"And he doesn't know?"

"That shit for brains is clueless what it takes to live on the outside. It's why he's spent so much time locked up. He likes it."

"Right now, he's up against a murder rap."

"He said something about that last time we spoke."

"Mazy, how long have you been with Keeney?"

"Forever. We been together since high school."

"Do you remember him breaking into a Regency house a year or so ago?"

She nodded her head.

"Do you remember if he said anything about it?"

"That was some fucked-up shit."

"Why? What'd he say happened?"

"He said that the woman was still alive. He was gonna call the police, but the husband came home, so, Keeney, he hightailed it outa there."

"Did Keeney say whether Bridgeton saw him?"

"He didn't think so, but he wasn't sure."

"Thanks, Mazy."

AFTER LEAVING MAZY'S with full knowledge that I wasn't getting paid, I checked messages. The Lab called. Dawn Ryker said she wasn't finished examining the knife and would get back to me, soon. I wasn't getting anywhere fast with the gifts Alec Covington left me. So far, I had photos from Savannah's crime scene that didn't match the official file, her finger, and the knife. Meanwhile, I was dodging my father's calls. When we did speak, I avoided anything having to do with Alec Covington. My father knew about everything except the knife. I didn't see the usefulness in telling him. I still had one more card to play. The Lab could access Savannah's original autopsy report and that's exactly what I asked Dawn to do.

The rumbling from my stomach sounded like a small-engine plane preparing to race down a runway. On the off-chance Michael Mathews might be available for lunch, I gave him a call. His assistant said that he'd stepped out and was kind enough to tell me where I'd find him. I was surprised she was willing to divulge his whereabouts, but she explained that he'd left instructions to tell me, if I happened to call. He was having lunch at Jams on Dodge Street. It was in the same strip mall as Zio's Pizzeria.

When I arrived, servers hurried table to table taking and delivering orders. I searched the small, narrow space for Michael; he had chosen a table along the wall. I wasn't sure what made me decide to pursue him. Nothing good would come of it. I mean, he's a millionaire who doesn't really know who I am. You can't build the foundation of a relationship on a series of lies and expect it not to get swallowed by the earth around it. And yet, here I was knowing full well that I wasn't at Jams to get information out of him. At least nothing related to Keeney's case. He was reading when I approached his table. It was set for two and a bottle of wine waited to be poured.

"Are you expecting someone?"

He looked up from his book, smiling. "Just a beautiful, brown-eyed girl. Have you seen her?"

I pulled out the chair next to his and sat. "What are we having today?" I said, gesturing to the wine.

"The 2011 Sterling Vineyards Merlot." He filled our glasses as a server delivered wings to the table. When she left, he laughed, saying, "What? I can't order hot wings for lunch?"

"You don't seem like the type of guy who'd order something so messy."

"Au contraire, Ms. Jackson, I love getting messy."

At that moment I realized the conversation had turned in a direction I needed to stay clear of, so I dialed it back.

"This wine is fabulous. Great choice."

"It's nice, and perfect with these wings. I love Cajun spices."

"I take it you've ordered this before?"

"Several times. Cajun cuisine is among my favorites."

"Have you spent much time in the South?"

"As a matter of fact, I have a place in New Orleans."

"Really? Where?"

"The French Quarter. I purchased a bed-and-breakfast after Katrina and spend several weeks each year, there. Have you been?"

"A few times. It's an interesting place."

"That it is. It's got a rich history, beautiful architecture, and wonderful people. I look forward to my stays very much."

He offered the plate of wings to me, and I couldn't resist. He was right about the pairing. After eating few pieces each, we settled back. The server returned, took our orders, and we sat in silence for a few minutes.

"You know, Ms. Jackson, you could have told me who you are."

I perked up.

"I did a little checking around and discovered that your specialty isn't freelance writing."

"Would you still have spoken to me?"

He leaned forward, his gaze unwavering, and said, "I find you intriguing."

A shiver, or maybe an electric charge, went straight up my spine. I could feel the heat in my cheeks. I reached for my water glass and drank.

"What do you really want to know?" he asked.

"James Keeney has been charged with your sister, Sarah's, murder. He hired me to see whether I can prove that he didn't do it."

"And can you?"

"I don't know, yet. I do know that a few things don't seem right."

"I don't believe this man, Keeney, killed my sister. I think he was burglarizing their house, got spooked, and ran."

"Why do you believe that?"

"When the police told me about Mr. Keeney, I hired an investigator to check into things. Mr. Keeney has never hurt anyone. My investigator thinks someone else came into the house that night and Mr. Keeney ran." He reached into his lapel pocket and handed me a card. "This is my investigator."

"Dick Swan?"

"Do you know him?"

"Only his reputation."

DICK SWAN INVESTIGATIONS was in Midtown. He'd been a PI for at least twenty years and was a retired homicide detective who had a reputation for following the rules that suited him, which is how he got booted from the force. I'd never met him, and really didn't want to now, but there wasn't any denying his uncanny ability to read a scene or situation with clarity and accuracy. He worked alone in an old building that'd been partially renovated into office suites. When I walked in, he was on the phone, but waved at me to take the seat in front of his desk. I didn't, and instead chose to lean against the wall to the right of the door.

"You tell that shit for brains – What? I don't give a rat's ass. He needs to get his ass outa there before nightfall." He ended the call and looked at me, smiling. "Dezeray Jackson."

I returned the smile with a nod.

"I've heard interesting things about you since you landed back in Omaha."

"Oh, yeah?"

"Yeah. Seems you're partial to working with the underbelly of society."

"Really?"

"Katrina? Mad Dog? Pearly Santos? Stop me when any names ring a bell."

Sarcasm. He was my kinda people.

"I do what works. That should be familiar to you from what I understand."

He leaned back in his chair with his hands laced behind his head.

"I gotchya. So what brings you here?"

"Michael Mathews mentioned that he hired you to check out James Keeney."

"And?"

"And I'm working for Keeney. I'm about ninety-five percent certain that he didn't have anything to do with Sarah Bridgeton's murder."

"Only ninety-five percent, huh? Well." He pushed back from his desk, got up, walked to a file cabinet, shuffled through a series of files, and then grabbed one. "I'm a hundred percent sure he didn't." He handed the file to me.

"What's this?"

"Let's just say that I was able to procure copies of the original investigation."

"What in here proves that Keeney didn't do it?"

"I'm still checking that out. Review the file. I added a few notes, from things I've learned. You'll notice that our buddy, Bridgeton, wasn't completely up front about his whereabouts." He returned to his desk and sat.

"Wait. The reports I read, and his partner, Myers, said that he was with Bridgeton at a client meeting."

"Nope. Not exactly."

I quickly scanned his notes; then I saw it.

"He was with a woman."

Swan nodded his head.

"Do you know who?"

"I haven't tracked her down. Yet."

"Does Mathews want you to?"

"Anything I can find that sheds a negative light on Bridgeton will make my client a happy man."

"Maybe we can work together."

"I don't take on partners."

"Neither do I. All I'm suggesting is that we keep each other informed."

"I suppose we can do that."

I left, feeling more satisfied about not getting paid for this gig. Ultimately, it's all about people getting what they deserve. I wasn't sure whether Bridgeton, or someone else, deserved a life sentence, but I did know it wasn't Keeney.

KEENEY SHUFFLED INTO the room wearing tennis shoes instead of the required black boots and sat across from me. The dark circles beneath his eyes hadn't diminished since we last spoke.

"What's with the shoes?"

Keeney smirked and said, "Bunion."

"Ah. Well, I think we might have something to go on."

"Whatya find out?"

"For starters, Cal Bridgeton is a womanizing, misogynistic pig."

"That ain't so bad. What else ya got?"

"He'd had several flings and affairs during his marriage."

"So? Ain't everybody?"

I took a deep breath and reminded myself that he was my client. Smacking him upside the head right about now wouldn't help his situation; I'd feel better, but I needed to stay focused.

"The point is that the police couldn't find evidence connecting him to his wife's murder, but they also didn't know that he was cheating on her. This means that there are possibly several other people who could've killed Sarah Bridgeton that night."

"Yeah, yeah, I see what yer sayin. It coulda been him."

"Maybe. I don't know for sure, but I do know that we have more to work with than we did a week ago. I'll give what I discovered to your PD."

"Great. Thanks." He stood. "Mazy told me you stopped by her place."

"Yeah, about that," I said, standing to deal with the proverbial elephant in the room.

"I know, she told me. But I can pay ya."

I held up my hand to stop him from continuing.

"Really, Ms. Jackson, I got more money. Mazy just don't know about it. If I gave her everything I got, the woman would spend it on all kindsa shit."

"Where's the money?"

"I got me a storage locker."

"And how am I supposed to get inside this locker?"

"It's an easy lock for someone like you."

Keeney gave me the address and I headed back to Omaha. I wasn't planning on visiting the locker tonight. Whatever he had in there could wait a day or so.

DINKLE SELF STORAGE was a fifty-bay facility in southeast Omaha, on South Thirteenth Street, in an area best visited during daylight hours. A chain link fence surrounded the property and the entry gate had been knocked off its hinges. There weren't cameras, and I doubted the lighting would be any good, judging by the bits of broken glass I saw on the ground beneath several poles, as I pulled into the driveway. I drove around the first row of bays to the second, and spotted Keeney's locker.

The place was a ghost town. I parked my Jeep, grabbed one of my larger tactical flashlights and my lock-picking tools. I set the flashlight on the ground while I inspected the lock. Keeney was right. I had it opened in about thirty seconds. I guess he wasn't too concerned about what was in his locker. I tossed the padlock to the ground, snatched up my flashlight and pulled the locker door up. A pile of boxes along the left side, a couch, TV cabinet, and kitchen table near the back nearly filled the space. To my right was a gun cabinet; I checked the handle. The damn thing was locked, and chances were, the money was inside. Damn Keeney. I spent the next fifteen minutes working on the cabinet lock. I only had a few tries to get it unlocked before it would freeze up and I'd be sitting for an hour before I could try again.

"Can I help you?" The gravelly voice of a longtime smoker jolted me from my concentration. I turned to see an old, heavyset, pale man with a comb-over and bad teeth standing at the entrance to the locker.

"No, not really."

"This ain't yer locker, is it?"

"No, it's my friend's. I'm just getting something for him."

"Who might that be?"

"James Keeney."

"Ah. He sent you, did he?"

"Yeah, he did. Look, if you don't mind, I'm kinda in the middle of something here." I turned away, thinking he'd get the hint and shove off.

"He said you might be by."

I stopped working the lock and turned to face the man. "Did he, now?"

"Yep. Said you might need this." He handed me a Post-It note with the combination to the lock. "Make sure you lock the unit up before you go."

I nodded and he left as quietly as he'd arrived. The man had ninja skills. He probably had some cool back-story, like spending years training in the Far East after the Vietnam War, and then he returned to the US to make his fortune, but then things went south.

Fortunately, the cabinet didn't have any guns or ammo. It contained a few files and smaller cardboard boxes. Keeney was a friggin pack rat. I found a box of one-hundred-dollar bills tied in bundles of ten. He had thirty grand in this one box. I took two bundles and replaced the box. There were three more boxes just like the first. Then I noticed a small book on the floor of the cabinet and knelt to pick it up. It was a journal. I had a hard time believing Keeney would keep a diary, so I flipped through it.

The first entry was about three years ago. The writing had a feminine flair to it. She wrote about not being able to trust some people around her. I skipped several entries. She mentioned meeting her sister for lunch to talk about her husband. She'd learned that he was having an affair but didn't know with whom. I flipped several more pages to what appeared to be the final entry dated September 9, 2014.

Cal doesn't know that I know. I haven't told Michael, yet, but when I spoke to Michelle, she denied it. Called me crazy for even thinking it, but I know it was her. I'm going to confront Cal.

Holy shit! He was having an affair with Sarah's sister. He's a special kind of asshole, that's for sure. Who the hell does that? And what the hell was wrong with Michelle? But none of this meant he or Michelle killed Sarah, so as excited as I was to have a glimmer of confirmation that the two were connected, I still had work to do. I closed the cabinet, went outside, and tossed my gear and the journal onto the passenger seat. Then I rolled the locker door back into place and secured the unit. I wondered whether Keeney read the journal or spoke to Sarah when he saw her that night. It looked like I was headed back to The Pen.

"SHIT, KEENEY, WHAT happened to you?" He was moving slower than molasses in winter as he entered the room.

"Ah, this?" He gestured to his face. His left eye was blackened and his lip split. "It ain't nothin. Just a misunderstanding." He winced when he pulled out the chair to sit.

"If you say so."

"What ya got?"

I showed him the journal. He picked it up and thumbed through it.

"What about it?"

"It belonged to Sarah Bridgeton. Why didn't you mention it before? Does your PD know about it?"

"I forgot all about it. What's the big deal?"

"The big deal is that Sarah wrote that Cal was having an affair. And from what I understand, it was with her sister, Michelle."

"Well, aw right, then!" He clapped his hands. "You got somethin. They sure as hell can't pin her murder on me, right?"

"Slow down. I've identified another possibility, but there's still the problem of finding your DNA at the scene, and nobody else's except who'd they expect. According to what we know, you were the only intruder that night."

"Yeah, but this is still somethin.'"

"Yeah, it is."

"What now?"

"I'll give my new information to your PD. And I'll keep searching. Just remember the fact that Bridgeton was having affairs means there are plenty of suspects I haven't found. Somebody could have hired a professional for all we know." The minute the words left my mouth, they felt right. This was a murder-for-hire job. I'd bet my fee on it.

As I walked to the door to leave, I turned back and asked, "Keeney, why'd you take the journal?"

"'Cause she asked me to."

"Sarah asked you to take it?"

"Yeah. She said it was in her study. I was in there gettin it when I heard someone come in, so I hightailed it outa there."

"Where'd you get out?"

"The kitchen. Her study was near the kitchen."

I left Keeney and returned to Haithem's office at Tracer International. Dalton was waiting for me when I exited the elevator.

"Did you put some sort of tracking device on me?" I asked as I passed him. He followed me into the office. I tossed my leather satchel onto a chair and sat behind the desk.

"A tracker? No, Ms. Jackson. I wouldn't do that."

"I was kidding, Dalton. What's that?"

He handed me a small package. "It came for you this morning."

I thanked him and he closed the door on his way out.

The package was a small priority box with no return address. Since it arrived at Tracer, I was confident that it didn't contain anything hazardous. The mailroom scans every box or large envelope entering the building. Inside the box, and on top of several pictures, there was a note from Haithem. He reminded me to check on his bird; It was with his parents. Translation: Make sure his parents are all right. I removed the pictures and spread them across the desk. Most of them were of a shipping area around Abaci Transportation Corporation. A few zoomed in on building numbers. I flipped over each picture to see whether Haithem had included any notes. On the backs of the ones with numbers, he'd indicated that those buildings contained explosives and other weapons. Now we had proof that Abaci Transportation Corporation was a front, but for whom?

CHAPTER FOUR

IT'D BEEN A FEW DAYS since I spoke with Charlie, so I tapped his number into my phone and waited for him to answer. After a few rings, he picked up sounding as if he'd just run a marathon.

"Are you all right?" I asked.

"Who's this?"

"Dez."

"Oh, yeah. I'm fine. Just give me a second to catch my breath." I heard a crackle and popping sound, then, "Shit. Mother Fu—."

"This a bad time?"

"No, no. Sorry. I dropped my phone."

"What are you doing, or don't I want to know?" Charlie and I handled a few cases together in Miami for Tracer. He was dependable, loyal, and could hit a mark with his knife from nearly a hundred feet away. No world record, but damn close.

"My client has me going all over New Orleans looking for this cat, Beautemps. Every time I think I've got a bead on him. Poof! He's gone. I'm starting to believe he's a figment of her imagination."

"How much do you know about your client?"

"Enough to know I don't want to get on her bad side, that's for damn sure. She's one of them old-time people. Practices voodoo and shit like that."

"There still a lot of that in New Orleans? I thought it was mostly for the tourists."

"She doesn't do the tourist circuit. She's strictly old school. Has a place in Algiers Point. There's always someone on her doorstep getting gris-gris when I stop by. She's got to be at least eighty, maybe older."

"I met a lady like that when I first returned to Omaha. Man, she scared the crap out of me. And you know that's sayin something."

We'd been in some precarious situations dealing with Miami's drug lords and none of that was as scary as Mayville Toussaint. She did stuff that defied logic.

"I've got a mind to give her the down payment back so I can be done with this mess."

"What'd this Beautemps guy do?"

"I don't even know. She just wants him located." Charlie started coughing. "Hold on." All I heard was sputtering and hacking, and then, "Your girl, Michelle's, been enjoying her stay in the New Orleans, that's fo' show."

"How's that?"

"She's been making the rounds to the local hot spots in the Quarter. So far, she's hit up Fritzel's, The Spotted Cat, Sweet Lorraine's, and Monteleone. She's got good taste in music."

"Anything else?"

"She did stop by a bed-and-breakfast place called Le Coeur, near the Quarter, but only stayed a hot minute. So far, I'd say your girl is being a tourist."

"All right. Just let me know if something changes."

"You got it!"

I missed working with Charlie. He always kept things interesting. Someday soon I'd have to visit him in New Orleans and see what kind of trouble we could get into.

MICHAEL MATHEWS CALLED Friday afternoon and asked me out for dinner and dancing. Against my better judgment, I said yes. Now I was in my room trying on dresses. I couldn't wear the same little black dress he saw me in at the fund-raiser. I finally settled on a deep purple, A-line cocktail dress with drop shoulders and simple detailing along the top, with a matching hemline. We agreed to meet at the Omaha Press Club, downtown. It's a private dinner club at the top of the First National Bank at Sixteenth and Dodge Streets. From there, we'd decide where to go dancing.

I entered the building and saw Michael waiting just inside the doors. His streamlined navy suit, and polka-dot blue silk tie accented his eyes and complemented his tanned complexion.

"Dazzling," he said as he approached and extended his elbow. "Shall we?"

He led me to the elevator. We stepped inside and rode to the top. It'd been years since I'd been to the Press Club, and back then it was part of some special event for military families. The host welcomed us and invited us to enjoy a drink at the bar while we waited for our table. We walked past a large fire pit in the center of the space and found seats at the bar, with a view of downtown Omaha. It didn't compare to the view at the top of The World Trade Center's Windows on the World, but it would have to do. We settled into the comfortable chairs.

Michael hadn't failed me yet in his wine selections, so I sat back and waited for him to read the wine menu. He ordered a Chardonnay and shrimp cocktail. Satisfied, he sat back, and turning his chair to face mine, he said, "It's not the New York City skyline, but it's getting there."

"New York City?"

"Isn't that where you were before returning to Omaha?"

Okay, that's creepy.

"You've done your homework."

"Only a little, I promise. Dick mentioned it, that's all."

"Uh, huh."

"Honestly, I'm not trying to secretly learn everything about you. I'd rather find out slowly. And from you."

A chill went up my spine. This was either going to be the most intense date I'd had in years, followed by mind-blowing sex, or an utter debacle. I was pulling for the former. The host interrupted our exchange to escort us to our semiprivate table. On three sides a high, teal-blue booth shielded us from other guests. Michael invited me to sit in the booth while he sat opposite me in a chair. This gave me the best view of the area, so I was comfortable and secure. A short time later, our appetizer arrived.

"Michael, since we're talking business..."

"Are we? I certainly don't mean to. I'd rather know more about you."

"Your sister, Michelle, is in New Orleans."

His reaction would have been easy to miss if I hadn't recently been studying and refreshing my mind about microexpressions. A flash of worry or concern registered on his face. I didn't know why, but it was worth following up.

"You seem concerned."

He shook his head, and then said, "No, I just didn't realize she had returned from her last trip."

"Does she spend much time in New Orleans?"

"Some, I suppose. She seems to prefer hot environments, so I guess I'm not surprised she went south."

"Maybe she wanted to see your new B&B? Does she know about it?"

"Oh, sure." He sipped his wine, set down his glass, and said, "Shall we order?"

I reviewed the menu, and asked, "What looks good to you?"

"Besides you, I'm considering the Steak Diane." He didn't even look at me when he answered. Smooth. Very smooth. "What are you thinking about having?"

"Something light. Maybe the blackened salmon. We are planning to go dancing, remember?" I reminded him.

He closed his menu and set it to the side. "Yes, we're definitely going to be dancing later." His gaze fell on mine and lingered.

Now, I was pretty sure we weren't talking about the same thing. "Does this usually work for you?"

"What?"

"The sexual innuendo."

"Is it?"

"A little, but it's a bit of a hard sell coming from such a seemingly strait-laced guy like you."

"Damn. And here I thought I was pulling it off."

"That comes later." I grinned and reached for my wineglass.

A FEW DAYS AFTER MY date with Michael, I made another appointment to speak with Cal Bridgeton. I was surprised he was willing to see me, but you know what they say about a gift horse and everything. He asked me to meet him at Nebraska Elite Sports and Fitness Complex on N.102nd Street, not far from Westroads Mall. I arrived at eleven o'clock.

One of the staff members pointed me toward a lounge area and paged Bridgeton. A short time later, Cal Bridgeton entered the lounge, toweling the sweat from his face. Before joining me at a table, he'd bought a Gatorade.

"Ms. Jackson," he said after he sat opposite me. "Why are we meeting, again?"

"Some new information came to light and I wanted to run it past you."

"New information about Sarah's murder?"

"No, new information about you."

He placed the bottle of Gatorade between us on the table, leaned into his chair and folded his arms.

"Do tell. I'd be fascinated to hear your discoveries."

"Why did Mr. Mathews turn on you? When you and Sarah began dating, and even during the first few years of your marriage, he appeared to like you. Even supported your business from what I understand."

His expression told me that he was surprised that I knew about his father-in-law's financial assistance.

"We had our differences, as in-laws sometimes do, but we respected each other."

"That's interesting."

"How so?"

"Take a look at these," I said, and laid out copies of several pictures of the two men together. "You know what I find so fascinating about these pictures?"

"Please, enlighten me."

"Take these for instance." I grouped five of them. "You see how close you're standing to each other. And in each of these you're either laughing or smiling. That smile is called a Duchenne smile. Actors do a pretty good job of faking it, but the average person, you know, like you, me, or Mr. Mathews here, we can't fake this so great. If we do, it looks more like..." I gathered the remaining handful of pictures and placed them in front of Bridgeton.

"This." I pointed to the first image.

"What is the point of all this? I've got things to do."

"I checked the dates for these pictures. The ones where you and Mathews are genuinely happy being next to each other were taken between 2010 and the summer of 2012. The rest of these were all taken after that. Don't you think it's interesting that he's obviously distancing himself from you in these?" I pointed to the second pile, again. "And check out your smiles. They're different, right? I'm not just making this up. You see it, right?"

"Ms. Jackson, the firm was experiencing a setback around that time. It would have been difficult to smile then."

"Oh, really? I thought maybe it had something to do with Mr. Mathews discovering that you were sleeping with another woman while you were married to his daughter. But maybe I'm wrong."

His jaw tightened and his lips pursed. I'd seen that expression before. He pushed his chair from the table to stand.

"As I said, Ms. Jackson, I have things to do." Without a glance back in my direction, he walked away.

I gathered the pictures and returned them to my satchel. One of my favorite aspects of my job is putting someone on the defensive. It gets them to do some crazy shit sometimes, but usually whatever they do ends up helping me. Now I just needed to sit back, watch, and wait for Bridgeton to make his move.

I'd also scheduled a meeting with Sam Myers for today and planned to meet him at his office. He knew more about Bridgeton's lust interests, and I needed names. A detail-oriented guy like Myers probably kept notes just in case he'd need them as leverage later. Pushing him during our first meeting didn't seem prudent. But now I had to twist some nickels. I checked the clock on a nearby wall. It was too early to meet him, so I left to get something to eat.

DANIEL GREETED ME WHEN I exited the elevator and told me that Myers was ready for our meeting. Sam Myers' office was to the left of the elevator and at the end of the hall. As I walked the length of the corridor, I passed several smaller offices. One belonged to a twenty-something blond, and I couldn't help but wonder whether some of the women Bridgeton had affairs with worked for him. It would be stupid, but people have office affairs all the time. They take the "office-spouse" idea one step further than they should.

Myers' door was open, and since he was expecting me, I didn't knock. He was standing near a fax machine reading something he'd apparently just received.

"Mr. Myers?"

"Ms. Jackson, please, come in and make yourself comfortable." He gestured to a seating area near a bank of windows with a view of more buildings. "Can I have Daniel get you anything?"

"No, thank you. I just came from lunch." I waited for Myers to join me. He'd returned his attention to the fax.

"Are you sure this is a good time?"

"Yes, yes. I just need to make a quick note and I'll be right with you."

After he'd finished reviewing the paper and making his notes, he grabbed a Coke that'd been on his desk, opened it and poured its contents into a coffee mug.

"It's my one indulgence. I don't know what they put in Coke, but I'm hooked." He walked over and sat in a chair across from the couch where I was seated.

"I think it's the burn," I said. "I'm hooked, too."

He smiled politely, then said, "So, how may I help you, today?"

"Mr. Myers, I got the impression the other day that you know more about Mr. Bridgeton's friends. And, to be honest, I'd like to know their names." Honesty. This was a new approach for me. Lying is a hell of a lot easier.

"As I told you, I don't really keep track."

He said, "really," which meant that he actually does keep track, but doesn't want to show his cards for some reason. Anytime I've ever said it that way, I was most definitely keeping track of whatever the hell was going on around me.

"Mr. Myers, I can appreciate your position, but I'm trying to make sure an innocent man doesn't end up spending the rest of his life in prison."

"You're talking about that man, James Keeney?"

"Yes. He's a low-level B&E guy, not a killer. He deserves to complete his current sentence. There's no question about that. But trying to pin a murder on him, well, I can't let that happen."

"B&E?"

"Breaking and entering. Keeney's known for that. And he has a particular way of doing it that never involves anyone being around when he enters. Usually, he checks out his targets for a while before hitting them."

"Usually?"

"Yes, most of the time."

"But not all the time. It's possible that this was one of those times."

"It's possible, but unlikely, based on his priors. He's never been charged or convicted of a violent crime, or even possessing a weapon."

"What makes you believe knowing the names of Cal's friends is going to help this Mr. Keeney?"

"Showing that Bridgeton had affairs and providing evidence about whom they were with, gives Keeney's public defender credible reasonable doubt to present to the judge."

"If I give you any names and they get out, our firm could suffer hundreds of thousands of dollars' worth of damage. Clients don't appreciate drama. And neither do I."

"Look, your business can overcome a little temporary drama. We're talking about someone's life."

He sat back against his chair and remained quiet for a minute. His gaze settled over my shoulder, to the windows.

"Mr. Myers, your partner doesn't need to know that I got any information from you."

"He'll know. There's not much that happens in our firm that he doesn't eventually discover."

I was beginning to get the sense that Myers wasn't happy with their arrangement, but I had no idea why. I tabled the thought and asked again.

"Who was he seeing around the time of Sarah's death?"

He breathed deeply, and then said, "I know of two women. Sophie Donaldson and Kristy Briggs."

I jotted down their names.

"I told you before, just because he had affairs doesn't mean that he didn't love Sarah. He did. Cal is competitive and he has a strong appetite for winning. He doesn't always consider the costs."

"I guess that's what makes you good partners."

"Probably, yes. Is there anything else, Ms. Jackson?"

"No, thank you for the information."

After leaving Myers, I stopped by Daniel's desk.

"Is he in?"

"No, he had an appointment out of the office."

"What kind of appointment?"

"This one is a legit business meeting."

"Daniel, do you know anything about a Sophie Donaldson or Kristy Briggs?"

He shook his head, and asked, "Should I?"

"No. I was just following up on a lead. Thanks."

"Glad to help."

Back in my Jeep, I called Dalton and gave him the names of the two women. I knew he'd have details for me by the end of the day. From the Bridgeton & Myers' office, I headed to Simmons Martial Arts Academy to get in a quick workout.

SOPHIE DONALDSON LIVED in an apartment complex near 144th and Maple Streets. When I arrived, she buzzed me inside and I took the elevator to her fourth-floor apartment. I was a little surprised to find her home during a weekday, until she answered the door; her large, round stomach greeted me first.

"You must be Dezeray Jackson. Come in."

The apartment was your garden-variety one with white paint throughout and a neutral, not-quite-shag carpet. A couch, love seat and bigger than average TV filled in the living room. There wasn't a dining room, but a space just off the kitchen contained a small square table with two matching chairs.

"You said you wanted to talk to me about Cal Bridgeton?"

"Um, yes. You worked for him?"

"Not exactly. I was his trainer."

"Trainer?"

"Yes."

"How long ago was that?"

"Ages."

"When are you due?"

"A few more weeks and this baby's coming out."

"Ms. Donaldson, I'm sorry to have to ask you this, but..."

"Did I sleep with Mr. Bridgeton?"

I nodded.

"I'm ashamed to admit it, but yes. I was young, and stupid. He said he was unhappy and planned to leave his wife, but, of course, that was a lie."

"How long did the affair last?"

"About six months. They'd been married for about a year by then, I think. I don't really remember. When I think about it now, I feel like such an idiot. He was so charming."

"Did he say anything about his wife that stood out to you?"

"No. He mostly complained about her father. He hated him."

"Really? What'd he say?"

"Oh, I don't remember now, but I'm sure Cal wasn't sad when Mr. and Mrs. Mathews died in that accident a few years later. I mean, it was after our affair, but I do remember thinking that when I heard about it on the news."

"Do you think Mrs. Bridgeton knew about your affair?"

"God, I hope not. Ya know, at the time I honestly believed everything he said about her. But now, since she was killed, and all the articles and reports about how amazing she was." She shook her head and sighed. "I feel horrible. I know he was lying. I just can't believe I fell for his bullshit."

She adjusted on the couch to get more comfortable. "Oh! That was a good one."

"Excuse me?"

"The little one is kicking up a storm. He might have just cracked a rib."

"Are you all right?"

"I'm just kidding. My ribs are fine. It just feels like he's trying to break them, that's all. I take it you don't have any kids?"

"No."

I thanked Ms. Donaldson for her time and couldn't get out of there fast enough. I wasn't ready to catch a baby.

KRISTY BRIGGS WORKED for an engineering-and-design firm in downtown Omaha called Edge Engineering. From what I was able to learn about her, she worked as a hardware engineer. My knowledge of what that involved was pretty much limited to the job description. The receptionist let Ms. Briggs know that I had arrived, and I waited in a small conference room near the lobby. A woman with shoulder-length red hair and an average build entered the room. I guessed her age to be mid-thirties. She closed the door behind her.

"You must be Ms. Jackson." She extended her hand and then invited me to sit down. "How may I help you?"

"I'm investigating a case and have a few questions about your relationship with Cal Bridgeton."

"A case? What case?"

"My client has been accused of murdering Mr. Bridgeton's wife, Sarah Mathews Bridgeton."

"And you don't believe your client is guilty?"

"No, I don't."

"But you think Cal had something to do with it?"

"I don't know. I was hoping that you could give me a few insights." She turned her chair slightly away from me and crossed her legs. "Mr. Myers mentioned that you had a relationship with Mr. Bridgeton. Do you mind telling me the nature of that relationship?"

"I don't know how knowing that will help your investigation. Is Cal a suspect?"

"I'm just gathering information for my client's lawyer. The thought of an innocent man spending his life in prison doesn't sit well with me."

"What makes you so certain that your client didn't murder Cal's wife?"

"Ms. Briggs, I've been an investigator for a longtime and my BS meter is generally on point. I can appreciate your desire to be discreet about your relationship with Bridgeton, but you're doing so at the expense of an innocent person. Doesn't that bother you?"

"Well, of course, I don't want your client to suffer, but my understanding is that he's a criminal and already serving his sentence. It's not as though he's really an innocent person."

"Who told you about my client?"

She shifted in her seat, pushing it farther away from me by a few inches. I don't think she even realized that she had.

"Ms. Briggs?"

"Cal called me the other day and told me all about your investigation."

"You're still seeing him."

With nowhere to go and no way to deny it, she said, "Yes." Her cheeks flushed and she fidgeted with a pen she'd been holding.

"Were you seeing him while he was married?"

She nodded.

"When was that?"

"We met a few months before his wife was killed. Honestly, it was just supposed to be a fling. A one-nighter. But..."

"What did Cal do to get you to continue the relationship?"

"You've met him."

"Yeah, so?"

"That man can do things to my body that I'd never believed possible. Seeing him is always a pleasure."

This conversation was about to take a turn down a road I didn't want to follow, but I had to hear her out.

"Come again?"

"Look, I don't expect you to understand. Cal and I aren't close in the way he was with his wife. I never wanted that from him. He loved her, but sexually he needed more, and so did I."

Sometimes, like now, I wished that flashing "tell-me-anything" sign I wore on my forehead could be turned off.

"We're not exclusive, even now."

"So, it's purely a sexual relationship?"

"Yes. And for the record, Cal didn't have any reason to want to kill his wife."

"Why do you believe that?"

"As I said, he loved her. In every aspect of their relationship, he was perfectly happy."

"Except sexually."

"Right. Some people..." She uncrossed her legs and moved closer to me. "Some people need sex more than others. That's all."

"You're saying that the two of you have some sort of sex addiction?"

"I suppose if you want to get clinical about it, yes."

"Are either of you seeing a therapist for your—problem?"

"It's funny, we both were when we met at a meeting."

"What meeting?"

"Sex Addicts Anonymous."

"It doesn't seem to be working for you."

She scoffed at that. "When we met, we decided that attending the meetings wasn't serving us well. Neither of us wanted to curb our desires. Not really. We wanted to be free to explore them more deeply with someone who understood what each of us needed. Cal couldn't do the things he does with me, to his wife."

"What are we talking about here?"

"We're completely uninhibited. With us, there aren't any boundaries. Normal sexual relationships can be so confining."

"Are you saying that he didn't have a sexual relationship with his wife at all?"

"He did, but he wasn't satisfied. In the beginning we met several times each week, but that wasn't enough; then we decided to meet several times a day."

"But you stopped seeing him at some point?"

"Only briefly. He became preoccupied with someone else."

"That must have been difficult for you."

"Not at all. As I said, we've never been exclusive."

"Do you know who the other woman was, or if he's still seeing her?"

"I don't know who she was, but I don't think he's seeing her now. His latest interest is someone in his office, but she's not like us."

"What makes you say that?"

"Recently, we've been seeing each other more frequently. If she were more like us, he wouldn't need me as much as he does."

"How do you know he's seeing someone in his office?"

"I stopped by after closing one evening and discovered them in her office."

"And that still didn't bother you?"

"No, I stayed for a while and watched."

"But I thought you said she wasn't like you."

"She was uncomfortable at first, but when Cal began kissing and caressing her body, she forgot I was there. He can have that effect on women. After I pleasured myself, I left."

"Well, thank you for your candor."

We both stood. I needed to get out of the room. I always thought of myself as pretty free-spirited sexually, but not anymore. Damn. In all my years, I'd never met a sex addict. I had met people into sadomasochism, but they weren't actually sex addicts. I kind of always thought it was some sort of joke.

Clearly, I was wrong.

"If there's anything else I can help you with, give me a call." She took a business card from her jacket pocket and handed it to me. "You're wasting your time investigating Cal. Trust me."

CHAPTER FIVE

"SEX ADDICTS? YOU'RE shittin me?" Dick Swan sat behind his desk drinking a beer. It was late afternoon and I'd stopped by to see if he'd discovered anything new about Bridgeton, Myers, or the mysterious woman. "Sounds like the mystery lady is this Briggs gal."

"I think so. But he had been seeing another woman at the same time and I think it was Michelle."

"Michelle? As in the vic's sister?"

I nodded.

"That's just wrong. He was sleeping with both of them and Briggs?"

"Well, it seems that his relationship with Sarah wasn't all that sexual. And if he really is a sex addict, then he's going to bang anyone who comes his way, right?"

"Looks like. But why would Michelle do it?"

"That's a good question. Has Michael ever talked about Michelle and Sarah's relationship?"

"According to him, they were close."

"What if he can't see their relationship for what it was?"

"Go on."

"Lots of siblings don't get along but learn to hide it around their families."

"I don't know. He seemed certain."

"Sarah kept a diary."

He took a long pull from his beer and set it back onto his desk. "Well, that's an interesting development. Do you happen to have the diary?"

"Yep. She wrote about meeting with Michelle and accused her of having an affair with Bridgeton. She planned to confront him. Michelle apparently denied the affair."

"When was this confrontation supposed to have taken place?" Swan asked.

"I'm not sure, but she was killed about two weeks after that entry."

"How'd you get the diary?"

"Keeney had it. Sarah spoke to him before he ran."

"That doesn't get us to the why. We need to track down Michelle."

"Already have. She's in New Orleans. A former associate is keeping an eye on her for now."

"What's your next move?"

"I don't want to travel to New Orleans to talk with her. There's got to be a way to get her to return to Omaha."

"You could say that Keeney's PD needs to talk with her about the case. She might be willing to cooperate even if she was pissed at her sister."

"It's worth a try." I headed toward the door to leave, but then turned back to ask, "What are you going to tell Michael?"

"Nothing, yet. He doesn't need to know about what Michelle may or may not have done with Bridgeton, and telling him about the sex addiction thing, well, that serves no purpose."

"All right. We're on the same page, then. I'll get back in touch."

OUTSIDE OF SWAN'S OFFICE building, my phone vibrated, and I saw that Dr. Roberts had left me a message saying I could pick Godfrey up from the clinic. He'd started eating, could keep it down, and was moving around, so there was no reason to keep him. When I arrived at the clinic, the assistant went to the back to get Godfrey. He entered the hall, saw me, and charged through the narrow corridor. When he reached me, he jumped up onto his hind legs. His front paws rested on my shoulders, and he licked my face.

"Oooo, Godfrey! Yuck!" I wiped my face with my forearm. "Glad you're feeling better." I rubbed his head and gave him a hug before pulling his paws from my shoulders and pushing him down. "I bet you're ready to go home."

He barked and his whole body shook excitedly. Dr. Roberts stepped into the hallway from one of the examination rooms, entered the lobby and shook my hand.

"He's out of the woods, but for the next few days, don't let him have any special treats. Just stick to his normal dog food."

"Will do. Thanks, Dr. Roberts."

"Call if anything changes. It was touch and go for a while there, but I'm anticipating a full recovery." He patted Godfrey on his head. "And Godfrey," Godfrey's ears perked up as he focused on the doctor. "Don't get into anyone's garbage or eat anything strange."

Godfrey hopped into the backseat of my Jeep, and we beat rush-hour traffic, making it home in record time. The first thing he did once we got into the house was make a beeline for the kitchen. He returned to the entryway with his food dish.

"Already? Okay, give me a sec." I kicked off my shoes, tossed my satchel onto the table near the door, and followed him back to the kitchen to fill his bowl. "Godfrey, it's good to have you back. The house was pretty quiet without you." I got interrupted by the phone ringing in my office and ran to answer it.

"Ms. Jackson?"

"Yes. How may I help you?"

"This is Sam Myers. I'm just calling to see if the information I gave you turned out to be useful."

"Yes, it was. Thank you. I appreciate that it made you uncomfortable to share it."

"My primary concern is the reputation of our business. We've worked hard to build it. I'd hate to see Cal's indiscretions disrupt our momentum."

"Is there anything else, Mr. Myers?"

"Were the ladies able to provide you with what you needed?"

"Yes, I believe so. Mr. Bridgeton went to see one of them the night his wife was murdered, so I think he has a pretty good alibi, if it should come to that, and as long as Ms. Briggs is willing to testify. I'm sure she would. They're still seeing each other."

"I see. That's good news. I mean, about him not having anything to do with Sarah's death. It's a relief."

"You were concerned?"

"You seemed very sure that it's not your Mr. Keeney. Who else could it be? I know that the police ruled Cal out, but that was because they didn't have all the personal details, I think."

"You might be right. Well, thank you, again, for your willingness to share the information with me. As I said, my objective is simply to help my client. I'm not trying to make anyone look bad in the process, least of all your company, Mr. Myers."

"I appreciate that. Have a good evening, Ms. Jackson."

The line disconnected and I returned to the kitchen to start making dinner.

I AWOKE TO THE MUFFLED snores of Godfrey at the end of my bed. He barely moved when I stroked his head, as I walked to the bathroom. It was a relief having him home; I'd underestimated how attached I'd become to the old police dog. When I'd returned to Omaha, this house felt big and empty compared to my apartment in New York City. One day, I was driving by the Omaha Humane Society and decided to stop. I told myself I'd just look at the small critters. I didn't think I could handle the commitment of a larger animal, even a cat, because I'd just relocated. The move was more hectic than I would have liked, partly because I was leaving someone in New York City who would have preferred that I stay.

After a quick shower and change, I was ready to tackle the day. I had to follow up with a few potential clients and meet with Keeney's public defender. I like to organize my days in the morning, but inevitably someone else's emergency becomes my next urgent matter.

I'd spent a few hours organizing, following up with clients, and scheduling meetings when I heard Godfrey amble down the stairs. The *click* of his nails on the hardwood floor let me know that he was headed to the kitchen. A few minutes later, he sat at the entrance to my office and stared at me until I got up and let him outside. I thought about installing a dog door, but I don't trust them, from a security perspective.

When I opened the door, I was face to face with Scott James.

"What the hell are you doing here?"

"We need to talk. Can I come in?"

"It looks as if you were about to do that anyway."

"No, I knew you were home."

"Really? How?" Hands on my hips, I was still blocking him from entering. "Shit, never mind, let me guess, you're still watching me?"

"Dez, can I come in?"

I stepped aside. His relaxed, fitted black khakis, and matching Polo shirt accentuated his physique. He set a black backpack onto the table. Then he removed a RF detector and a notebook.

"What's this all about?" I asked.

On the notepad, he wrote, "Someone's been tailing you. Did you know that?"

I didn't, and that detail pissed me off.

I mouthed, "Who? For how long?"

He removed a folder from his backpack that contained pictures of a man wearing some sort of black, military-style uniform. Scott began sweeping the kitchen for bugs. When he didn't find anything, he began moving room to room. In my office, he found one, but he didn't remove it. Then, he went upstairs; there was another one in my bedroom. Now I was seriously pissed. What an a-hole! I followed him back to the kitchen and into the basement. There weren't anymore. We returned to the kitchen. He grabbed his backpack but left the folder and we exited through the back door. We didn't stop walking until we were out of my backyard and into the alley. He motioned for me to follow him to the end of the gravel road toward the block south of my house.

"He's good. I haven't been able to get a clean shot of him, but from what I've seen he's about 5'10", maybe 190 pounds and some change. He's been on you for at least a few weeks."

"And you're just now telling me this because?"

"I wanted to see what I could find out before coming to you."

"And?"

"Nothing. I thought maybe he was connected to Alec Covington somehow, but it doesn't look that way. Whatever he's after, it's all about you." He paused for a minute, and then said, "I just wanted you to know."

"Well, thank you, but why the hell have you been keeping tabs on me, again?"

"You haven't exactly been speaking to me lately, but we still need to know what you find out about your sister's case, and we do know Murphy has Haithem holed up somewhere dissecting Abaci Transportation Corporation. We should all be working together, now. It'll make things easier."

"And you have no clue why this other guy is so interested in me?"

He shook his head. "If I did, I'd tell you."

"What should I do about the bugs? If I remove them, then he'll obviously know."

"I'd leave them in place for now. Since you know where they are, you can adjust your routine."

He slung his backpack over his shoulder. "I need to get going. Think about what I said." He handed me a small, folded piece of paper. "This is the best way to reach me." He turned away and disappeared around the corner.

I stood there for a minute, dumbfounded. Who the hell was this guy watching me? After running possibilities through my head, it occurred to me that it could be any dumbass I'd investigated over the past several years. I was going to have to narrow the field, somehow. But how? I returned to my house, let Godfrey outside, and gathered what I'd need for my meeting with Keeney's PD. There wasn't any use focusing on my new friend at this point. Eventually, like every other sneaky son-of-a-bitch I'd dealt with, he'd surface when he felt the advantage was his. I'd just have to be ready.

BACK IN OMAHA, I CALLED Michael. I needed to prod him more about what he might know about Michelle's supposed relationship with Bridgeton and get his help convincing her to return to Omaha for a meeting with Keeney's public defender. Sure, that part was a lie, but only a small one. Eventually, whatever useful information I learned from Michelle would land at the PD's office. Besides, in my experience people like being lied to more often than not.

I met Michael at his restaurant and found him in the same spot in the bar. It must be his table. He stood and gave me a quick hug before pulling out my chair so I could sit next to him.

"You're looking lovely, as usual."

"Thank you. I love your tie." The tie had an abstract, but colorful print.

"It was a gift from Sarah for Christmas a few years ago. I've always liked it, too."

A server stopped by our table with water, two wineglasses and a bottle of Merlot.

"I ordered the cheese and fruit plate this time just to change things up a bit," he said, smiling.

"What are we drinking tonight?"

"This wine is from the Rodney Strong Vineyard. I've always enjoyed their Sonoma County Merlot, so I make sure that we keep it in our selection. It's reasonably priced and not completely out of reach for the millennials who visit."

"You seem to have a better than average knowledge of wine."

"I've spent a little time visiting various vineyards in California and Washington, but I wouldn't consider myself an expert. When I find something, someone, intriguing then I want to learn everything I can about it, or them."

"And what happens when you're no longer intrigued?"

"I develop other interests, but so far that hasn't happened with wine."

"With women, then?"

He leaned closer, his fingers lightly touching the back of my hand. "I've found some women interesting, but not intriguing."

I broke his gaze and reached for my wineglass. The server returned and placed our appetizer onto the table. The chef included a small dish of dark chocolates. I set my glass down before picking up the conversation, again. Michael's arm rested on the back of my chair, so I angled it slightly forcing him to adjust and remove his arm.

"I take it this meeting is business not pleasure?" he asked.

"I learned something about Michelle, and I'm curious whether you can confirm it."

"What is it?"

"Was Michelle involved with Cal Bridgeton either before he met Sarah or during their marriage?"

Michael leaned against the back of his seat. His eyebrow furrowed and his jaw tightened, but it was fleeting. Then he said, "Michelle didn't meet Bridgeton.

None of us met him until he proposed to Sarah. She was very private about her relationships. We were all surprised when she brought Cal to dinner and made the announcement. It seemed out of character for her. Impulsive. I would have expected it from Michelle, but not Sarah. So, no, I don't think Michelle had an intimate relationship with Bridgeton before Sarah met him."

"How about after?"

"Bridgeton wasn't faithful to Sarah. We all knew that after my father caught him with his pants around his ankles at the office. But I suspect I'm not telling you anything you don't already know. Michelle and Sarah were close."

I sensed hesitation in his voice, and asked, "But something happened?"

"I don't know what it was. They grew distant about a year after Sarah married Cal, but I didn't think anything of it. I assumed that the marriage became Sarah's focus and thought that's all it was. I believed that Sarah and Michelle would eventually get back on track with each other."

"But they didn't?"

He shook his head. "If anything, they became more distant."

"Did either of them talk with you about the other?"

"No, not really."

"Do you know whether either of them kept a diary?"

"They did while we were growing up, but I don't know if they continued the practice as adults. Why?"

"I found a diary belonging to Sarah."

"What did it say?"

"She accused Michelle of having an affair with Bridgeton and she planned to confront him. Two weeks later, Sarah was killed."

The tension in his jaw returned.

"Are you saying that he had something to do with Sarah's murder?"

"I don't know. I discovered other details that provide him with an alibi, but I think it's possible that he might have hired someone."

He leaned forward and spoke in hushed tones. "Why? What reason could he possibly have?"

"The company was still young. Maybe he didn't think it could sustain a scandal. Taking Sarah out of the picture and making him out to be the poor, grieving husband would garner him sympathy, not criticism. From what I know of Cal Bridgeton, he's competitive and controlling. Oh, and a sex addict."

"What?"

"That was one of the things I discovered, and the woman he was with that night can provide him with an alibi."

"Why would Michelle have an affair with him? That doesn't make any sense."

"Sam Myers was seeing Michelle."

"Yes, I remember that."

"Myers told me that Bridgeton always wants what he can't have until he gets it. He's a sex addict. He sees Myers, who he's always been competitive with, dating Michelle. And now he wants her, too. It's a compulsion. He probably pursued her."

"That doesn't explain why she'd betray Sarah."

"You're right, it doesn't. That's why Keeney's public defender wants to speak with her. I was hoping you could contact Michelle."

"I didn't realize you were working for the public defender's office."

"I'm not, but this is something I told them about and it's an angle they can pursue to defend my client. Will you call her?"

Michael sipped his wine, returned the glass to the table, and said, "I don't want anything to happen to Michelle. She left because she couldn't cope with Sarah's death. Being away has helped her."

"Nothing will happen to her. No one even needs to know she's in Omaha." I tried to sound convincing. The truth was, I didn't know where Michelle was the night Sarah was killed. And I needed to know. The police didn't investigate anyone in the Mathews family beyond the usual suspects. For all I knew, she did it. Envy is a huge motivator, and it can make sane people do crazy things.

"Okay, I'll see what I can do."

It felt awkward to stay after that, so I made an excuse about needing to check on Godfrey and left.

THE LANCASTER COUNTY Public Defender's office is in Lincoln, NE, inside the Courthouse Plaza on South Ninth Street. I plugged a meter, knowing I wouldn't be long. Keeney's PD was a young woman named Marissa Clark. He'd originally been assigned to another young attorney named Bancroft something, but he was shot and in critical condition at Bryan Memorial Hospital. I'd learned this when I called to make the appointment. I didn't have, or more honestly, didn't want to know the details about Bancroft's shooting.

When I entered the space, the waiting area was packed with clients, or family members of clients. As I approached the receptionist, I noticed a woman seated to my left was crying, while a man comforted her. I didn't want to know their story, either. I gave the receptionist my name. About five minutes later, Marissa Clark introduced herself to me and invited me to her office.

"Thank you for coming, Ms. Jackson."

Marissa Clark was probably in her late twenties. Her office was smaller than the cell Keeney occupied. Her desk faced the door with two chairs across from it. A file cabinet stood in a corner to the right of the door, and the only personal touches were framed pictures of her degrees and certifications. My guess was that she either hadn't been here long or was mentally already on her way out. I was hoping it was the former.

I occupied one of the seats in front of her desk and removed a file containing the diary, and notes from what I'd discovered so far. I slid the folder across the top of her desk. "I think you might find some of this information helpful."

She opened the folder and her eyes widened.

"The diary belonged to Sarah Mathews." I went on to explain how Keeney ended up with it.

"And these women?"

"Cal Bridgeton is apparently a sex addict. You'd have to find some way to verify that. Ms. Briggs didn't know the therapist's name. But she confirmed that he was with her some time before he arrived home that night."

"Well, this just helps rule him out as a potential suspect."

"Maybe."

"What are you thinking?

"He could have hired someone to do it for him. I read an article that mentioned Bridgeton didn't call the police immediately after discovering his wife's body. Why would he wait?"

"Shock?"

"Or maybe he needed time to take care of something else."

"Like what?"

"I don't know. I'm just thinking out loud. But even if he had nothing to do with it, you've got the women to check out. And there's one more thing,"

She'd been thumbing through the diary and looked up.

"Bridgeton may also have had an affair with Sarah's sister, Michelle."

"Seriously?"

I nodded. "Check out the last entry in the diary."

She flipped to those pages, read them, and her face paled.

"Ms. Jackson, you've been a tremendous help. I don't know how Keeney found you, but he's lucky to have you on his side."

"We go way back." And by way back, I meant about a year when I caught him breaking into my house through a basement window. I'd just finished lugging boxes down there when I heard some strange noise coming from another part of the basement. When I went to check it out, Keeney was on his ass beneath the window. After I beat the shit of him, I called the police. He served a little time, but the judge went easy on him partly because of the beatdown I gave him, and it was his first time getting caught. Judge Barnes was amused by Keeney's misfortune to have encountered me that day. He got released for good behavior. I hadn't seen or heard from him since. When he contacted me from The Pen, I was surprised to get the call, but even more surprised that he wanted my help.

"If I find anything else that could be useful to your case, I'll let you know." I stood to leave. She followed suit and we shook hands.

"Thank you. If you need more investigative work, I'm sure we could use you."

Never one to turn down possibilities, I handed her my card.

From the courthouse, I headed to Haithem's parents' house to check on his parrot. Mrs. Nazari greeted me with a hug and welcomed me inside.

"Dezeray, you're looking lovely as usual, my dear."

I loved her accent. It was a little thicker than Haithem's and with a bit more of an Arabic influence.

"Mr. Nazari is working today. He's begun to provide translation services for the Arab refugees. The various social-service agencies don't have nearly enough volunteers and there are so many in need of help."

The Nazaris were educated at Oxford, spoke as many languages and dialects as their son, and had retired when they moved to Lincoln, NE, to be closer to Haithem. When they learned about his death, they decided to stay in Lincoln rather than return to England. Not being able to tell them the truth was painful, and when Haithem did come back, I wasn't sure how he'd handle things with them. Or if they'd forgive me.

"How's Phineas?"

I followed her into a large kitchen with a sunroom leading to a backyard garden reminiscent of something you'd see on Downton Abbey. Phineas was perched on the branch of a small, flowering tree.

"Hello, Phineas."

"Hello," he said.

"I brought you your favorite treat." I'd picked up a pint of blueberries on my way over and handed him one.

"Would you like tea, Dezeray?"

"Yes, thank you."

She returned to the kitchen and brought out a pot of what I knew would contain sweetened mint tea and a plate of small, wafer cookies. I always enjoyed visiting with Haithem's parents. I'd met them early in my career with Tracer, when Haithem and I went to England to pursue a man accused of embezzlement.

"And how are things with you?"

"Busy, as usual." I told her about Keeney's case.

"That's awful. That poor man."

"Well, to be fair, he isn't completely innocent."

"True, but if he didn't kill that woman, he certainly shouldn't be punished for it."

We continued our conversation, touching on various aspects of criminal behavior and US laws compared to other countries. I was so engaged, that I lost track of time. When I checked, two hours had passed.

"Oh, Mrs. Nazari, I really need to get going." I stood to leave, and she followed me back inside. "Here," I handed her the blueberries.

"Dezeray, don't be a stranger. You haven't come by for dinner in quite some time. I know that Mr. Nazari would enjoy seeing your smiling face. You and Haithem were always so good together." By together, she meant "couple" even though we'd never actually dated. His parents were very clear about whom they thought he should marry if he wasn't going to marry an Arab girl.

We hugged, and I assured her that I'd call soon about dinner. I'd have to be crazy to pass up a free meal that I knew was going to be homemade, and probably include lamb, hummus, flat bread, fresh labneh, grape leaves, and cardamom-scented rice. Mrs. Nazari was an amazing cook. She tried to teach me to make grape leaves once, but I kept tearing the leaves.

"IS THERE SOME REASON you didn't tell me about James contacting you?"

I was standing at the entrance to my kitchen being interrogated by Murphy, who had once again, let himself in uninvited. Godfrey happily gobbled pieces of chicken that Murphy had no doubt provided.

"He's not supposed to be eating anything except dog food." I pointed to Godfrey.

"Don't change the subject. Why didn't you tell me?" He went to the refrigerator and retrieved two Lucky Bucket IPAs. He popped the cap off both and handed a bottle to me. Murphy leaned against the counter waiting for me to answer.

"I didn't see the need."

"You didn't see the need? Really? This guy used you so he could get more information on Abaci Transportation Corporation. He got close to you."

"To be fair, he also gave me information about Savannah's case. Information that contradicted the police files. I wouldn't have anything more to go on if he—they, hadn't started feeding me those details."

Murphy and Haithem learned that Alec Covington was an ex-Marine who'd been killed after leaving the service. He was connected to Scott and three other former soldiers. Of the five in the original group, three were dead, including Alec. Every time I received something from them, it was signed with Covington's name, but we still didn't know exactly how or why he died. We only knew why they were using me. They assumed that my sister's case was somehow connected to someone they worked for, but they needed outside eyes on it. Someone who wasn't military, but who would be able to investigate Abaci Transportation Corporation. My former connections to Tracer International, and my more recent semi-permanent connection, provided me with a level of access to data that few beyond the military would ever have.

Lowering my voice, I said, "Scott came here to warn me."

"Warn you about what?"

I set my beer onto the table and motioned for him to follow me to my office. I located the bugging device and his eyes narrowed as he processed what he'd seen. Silently, he followed me upstairs to my bedroom where I showed him the second bug. We returned to the kitchen and out the back door.

"What the fuck is that all about?" he asked.

I shrugged.

"What'd James say?"

"He showed me a few surveillance pictures."

"Wait a minute. James hasn't stopped watching you?"

"Apparently not. Anyway, he had a few shots of a guy, but nothing clear. He's average height. Average build. And probably well-trained."

"What else?"

"Scott wants to work with us."

Murphy started pacing. That was never a good sign. His hands repeatedly balled into fists.

"I know Scott is on both of our shit lists, but if his crew is down to two, then he needs more support if he's going to find out what happened to Alec Covington. And we might be able to use them to find out who's been targeting you, and why they wanted Haithem out of the picture. You're the one who told me this was bigger than Savannah."

He stopped pacing and turned to look at me. "What about your new admirer?"

"There's not much I can do about him until he makes another move."

Murphy nodded his head. "If he comes anywhere near you..."

"I know. I can handle it, Murphy."

"Not if he, whoever he is, attempts to take you out from a distance."

Well, that was a comforting thought.

"We're getting ahead of ourselves. So far, all he's done is watch me for a few weeks and bug my house."

Murphy's eyebrows raised, causing creases to form along his forehead. It was one of those "are you really that naive" sort of expressions he liked to throw at me from time to time.

"What do you expect me to do?"

"You could stay at Haithem's apartment in Lincoln. The company still has it, right?"

"Another director is living there."

"You need to relocate."

"What about Godfrey? I'm not going to find too many temporary housing situations that allow a big dog."

"Get the higher-ups to make a few calls. One way or another, you need to get out of this house until we can get more intel on this new admirer of yours." He polished off his beer. "That's how James could really make himself useful right now."

"Come again?"

"He's already been watching the guy. Let's have him keep watching in exchange for us delivering more information about Abaci. He gets something. We get something. And I don't have to see him." Murphy returned to the kitchen. I heard the refrigerator door open, and then close.

"You want another one?" he asked.

"No. Murphy?"

He came back outside to the deck.

"How the hell did you know about Scott?"

"What are you talking about?"

"Don't play games with me."

He pulled out a chair, turned it around, and sat. His arms dangled over the top of it, one hand holding his beer.

"Shadow, remember?"

"I don't need a shadow."

"Clearly, love, you do."

"You can't keep risking your neck watching mine. We know someone's after you."

"You know me better than anybody. They aren't going to find me unless I decide to let them. It's not time for that."

"I don't want to stay at Haithem's place." I sat across from Murphy. Godfrey came over and nudged my leg, so I'd pet him. "The guy is following me. All he'll do is follow me there. At least here, I'm comfortable. Besides, with two wicked, ex-military dudes watching my ass, I'm feeling pretty good about my chances."

Murphy leaned forward, tilting his chair toward me. "And it is a nice ass." He wrapped his free hand around the back of my neck and kissed me long, hard, and deep. I felt tingling sensations from my nipples to my bajingo. It was going to be one of those kinds of nights.

Around eleven o'clock, I untangled from Murphy. He was sleeping on his stomach and moved a little when I got up, but then, settled again. I grabbed my silk robe and went downstairs to my office. Whoever was spying on me got an earful a few hours ago. That made me chuckle a bit. In all my years doing surveillance work, the worst was having to listen to people have sex, especially if that surveillance was with another agent.

I pulled out Savannah's file from a small rolling cabinet behind my desk. As I reviewed the contents, memories flooded into my head. When we were kids, all four of us were inseparable. Now my oldest brother was in New Orleans, and the other was in Denver. And Savannah and my mother were dead. My father seemed to have adjusted to my mom's passing. He was becoming more involved in his Baltimore neighborhood. He even opened a new dojang, and his consulting business was successful. But for me, a hit-and-run is as bad as an unsolved murder.

Thoughts of my sister, mother and me cooking up a feast in the kitchen just because we could, made a small smile spread across my face. That's when I stopped cooking. It was when Savannah was killed. My mom tried to get me back into the kitchen. But without Savannah, it just wasn't the same.

Godfrey's bark startled me from my thoughts. I reached into my top desk drawer, pulled out my gun and made sure it was loaded. I peeked around the corner of my office door and saw Godfrey, nose to the ground, growling at the front door. Murphy, half-dressed, barreled down the stairs, gun in hand. Finger to my lips, I signaled for him to be quiet and to go around back. Meanwhile, I watched the front-door handle for movement and eased closer to the bay windows for a look. When I moved the curtain, I saw Murphy with his hands around the back of Scott's neck, pulling him down the steps. Scott fought him off. I ran to the door, unlocked the bolt, yanked the door open and ran out into the yard.

"Murphy!"

The two men separated.

"What the hell are you doing here?" I asked Scott. "Shit. Let's go inside before the neighbors wake up and call the cops."

Once inside, I tossed a dishtowel at Scott so he could clean up the blood around his nose.

"I'm waiting," I said. Murphy, hands on hips, steadied his breathing and stared at Scott.

"I tracked our mystery man here. He did something to your Jeep, and before he could do anything else, I provided a distraction. That's probably what alerted Godfrey. And I found this on the ground. He must have dropped it." He tossed a small GPS tracker onto the table. "I was about to ring the bell when Murphy went ballistic." He turned toward Murphy. "What the fuck is wrong with you?"

"Oh, I don't know. Some strange guy is at my girl's house at midnight about to break in. What would you do? Consider yourself lucky I didn't break your fucking neck."

"Is that right?" Scott moved into Murphy's personal space. He had a few inches on him, but my money was on Murphy.

"Calm down and back the hell up." I got between them and pushed Scott back. "Jesus H. Christ, this isn't a pissing contest. Did you see what he looked like?"

"No. He was wearing a hoodie."

"You could have stopped him," Murphy said.

"Yeah, I suppose I could have, but then what? Drag him to Dez's doorstep? Get the police called? No, it's better if I track him and see who he might be connected to."

"Okay, then, keep tracking him, but stay the fuck away from Dez." Murphy walked out of the kitchen. I knew that if he didn't leave at that moment, he'd be all over him.

"I guess I should thank you," I said.

"Despite what you might think about me, Dez, I don't want anything to happen to you. And not just because of the Abaci deal." He moved closer to me, his hand reaching for my face. I stopped him.

"You don't have that privilege anymore."

He nodded, walked to the back door, and left. Godfrey, who'd been sitting on his bed watching, the hair on his back slightly raised, turned in circles, and then lay on his bed. I turned off the lights and met Murphy back in my bedroom.

CHAPTER SIX

MURPHY LEFT EARLY THE next morning, after checking my Jeep, and without rehashing the previous night's intrusion. As much as he hated Scott James, he admitted that having him around right now was a good thing. My feelings were mixed. I wouldn't describe them as hate. I was angry, but I believed him when he said our relationship wasn't simply an assignment. And having him show up last night proved to be a good thing. Murphy discovered that the gas line in my Jeep was cut. After arranging for a taxi, I got cleaned up.

The taxi dropped me off at Thrifty Car Rental at Eppley Airport. I picked up a silver two-door, Chevrolet Spark and headed to The Lab for a meeting with Dawn Ryker. She'd left me a message letting me know she had more information about the knife the Covington group had given me. After entering the secured facility, I walked the long corridor to the centrally located lab rooms. Now that I had Haithem's clearance level I could enter and exit the facility without an escort.

I stood behind glass walls observing Dawn Ryker examine a sword. When she saw me waiting, she waved and signaled that she'd be another five minutes. There wasn't any sense in wandering around, every hallway looked the same, so I stood there watching. It looked as if she was performing some sort of chemistry experiment, and I had no clue what it was. Then smoke began filling her lab. She grabbed a small extinguisher from a nearby table and put the fire out. No one else in the lab reacted. Dawn cleaned up her mess and met me in the hall.

"Let's go to my office. The knife is in there." I followed her through a few hallways to her office. She opened the door; the office was bathed in natural light. I looked up to see that a three foot by three-foot skylight had been installed in the roof.

"That new?"

She looked up, smiling. "Yep."

"I wondered how any of you could stand working in this place. Did everyone get one?"

"Yes, and it's making a huge difference already. I'd wither and die without the sun." She walked behind her large oak desk to a file cabinet, unlocked it, and reached inside. Turning to me, she said, "Here you go. I found a few latent prints. Turns out Godfrey's teeth didn't cause too much damage. There's one full right-index finger and two partials - thumb and pinky. My technician ran the prints, but he didn't find anything. You might see if someone in the Lincoln office can work their magic."

All of Tracer's best analysts worked in the Lincoln office. If someone was trying to hide or bury anything, one of our people could likely find it. True, it might take a little time, but at the end of the day, they'd have a conclusive answer to whatever question was posed.

"What kind of idiot leaves his prints on the murder weapon?" I was thinking out loud, but Dawn offered an answer, anyway.

"It's possible. If it were a mugging, the perpetrator wouldn't necessarily be organized. It might have been a last-minute decision."

"Or someone wants to lead me down a useless path. Finding actual prints seems too easy." I put the knife and her report into my satchel.

"Dez, it may not be anything, but you know you have to check out every angle. You'll be pissed at yourself if you don't."

She was right, of course. Dawn and I had gotten to know each other more since Haithem disappeared. I was handling all his case oversight at Tracer and much of it involved working with The Lab here in Omaha. I hadn't realized that before.

"What about the autopsy report? Have you found anything?"

"Still working on that. The report I located seems to be missing some information."

"Like what?"

"The examiner mentioned finding a small puncture wound here," She pointed to a spot on her neck just behind her left ear, but above the jawline. "But then the details aren't there."

"What do you mean?"

"Normally, I'd expect to see an explanation of the findings, but there isn't one. It's like the examiner simply went on to the next task, but I can't imagine why he would've done that."

"A small puncture wound? Like from a needle?"

"Probably, yes."

"What about the toxicology screen?"

"That's another strange thing. The report isn't complete. The toxicology screen is missing."

"But I saw the report. I have a copy."

"I'm not finding the toxicology report in any of the systems that I've accessed. Where did you get yours?"

I couldn't answer that truthfully without bringing in the Covington group. And that wasn't something she needed to know about.

Dawn Ryker would have been an excellent detective. Seeing the expression on my face that I wasn't able to tell her, she said, "Bring me a copy of the one you have. I don't need to know how you got it in order to read it."

"If my sister wasn't killed by the stabbing, and it was from something injected into her, what could it be?"

"There are several possibilities. If the killer had access to the combination of drugs typically used in death-penalty cases, then we're talking about pentobarbital, propofol, midazolam. Basically, it involves a stronger-than-normal dose of a drug to knock the person out, another drug to induce paralysis, and then a drug to stop the heart. But in an execution, these drugs are given in a specific sequence, not simultaneously. In your sister's case, if a drug was used, I would tend to believe that the killer would want a single drug that would have a similar desired effect as the ones I just mentioned, but without the need to inject her more than once. The autopsy report didn't mention any other puncture wounds."

I thanked Dawn for her time and left her office feeling agitated and frustrated. Knowing how Savannah was probably killed made me all the more determined to find the person responsible. And when I did, God help him.

As I walked to the parking lot looking for my Jeep, but not finding it, I immediately thought it'd been stolen. Given the previous night's activities, it was certainly a possibility. Then I remembered that I was driving a smaller than shit rental car. That realization didn't do anything to improve my mood. I knew one thing that would, though – shooting a few games of pool. It was still early, but I knew Eddy would be preparing for the lunch crowd, and I could eat a little something.

EDDY GREETED ME FROM behind the bar with a nod and asked, "You're kinda early, don't ya think?"

"I need a brain break," I said, as I pulled out a stool and tossed my satchel onto the seat next to me.

Eddy filled a glass with ice and water, then setting it in front of me he asked, "Lay it on me."

"The Lab found prints on the knife but can't match them to anyone. I need to have Dalton do that from Lincoln. And there's information missing from the autopsy report."

"What kind of information?"

"The toxicology report. There's also a distinct possibility that whoever killed Savannah injected her with something. Dawn Ryker, she's a researcher at The Lab, found a reference to a small puncture wound, but no other details. It doesn't make any sense." I sipped my water, then set it back down. "Why would the coroner's office file an incomplete report, and what happened to the tox screen?"

Eddy leaned his elbows onto the bar. "You know sometimes things just get lost from department to department. Shit like that happens more often than people want to believe. You remember that young buck last year who got beat up by those skinheads?"

I nodded.

"Then you must also remember how the video from the convenience store disappeared before the trial. Every day, Ms. D. Every damn day. So, you shouldn't be surprised it happened seventeen years ago."

A few customers came in and sat at the bar. Eddy walked away to get their order. I turned on my stool so that I could watch a few games and saw a familiar face at one of the tables. Clive Dixon was hustling someone. I could tell by the expression on his face and his "ah shucks" gestures that he was setting the other player up. Clive didn't learn from Eddy, like I did, but he still was a pretty strong shooter. If he ever decided to go legit, he'd make money on the tournament circuit. Well, unless he played me. Of course, since I'm not playing the circuit, he doesn't need to worry.

Eddy returned with a cheeseburger plate. "I assume since you're here at lunch you plan to eat?"

I turned to face him, already smiling from the fresh aroma of fries, onion rings and grease.

"Thanks, Eddy."

"You want a beer?"

"Yep."

A few seconds later I sunk my teeth into the greasy, cheesy goodness that could only be gotten at Eddy's. It was the best burger in Omaha. Hands down.

"What is your secret?" I asked, wiping my mouth, and reaching for my beer.

"If I told ya, it wouldn't be a secret, now would it? Just eat your burger and be happy." He snagged a few of my fries before walking away to refill water for the two guys who'd just come in. The cook chimed the bell that rested on the windowsill between the kitchen and the bar. Eddy grabbed the order and delivered it to the guys. Their conversation ceased as they took their first bites.

After a very satisfying last bite of my cheeseburger, I polished off the fries, onion rings and beer. I stood to stretch when Eddy returned with another beer.

"You planning to shoot?"

"Yeah, I'm going to see who's up for a game."

"Clive's been here about an hour. He's up a few hundred."

"That could be entertaining. It's been a while since I played him."

"Don't play nice. I taught you better than that."

I tossed my satchel strap over my shoulder and grabbed my beer before heading to Clive's table. He'd just finished his game and was pocketing a few twenties. He looked up when he heard me approach.

"Ms. D! How's it goin?"

I set my satchel onto the bar table, along with the beer, before walking past him to grab a stick from Eddy's rack on the wall. Not many people were allowed to do that, including Clive.

"What, you wanna play? You sure 'bout that?"

"Why not?" I asked, as I returned to the table and laid the stick atop it so that I could set the rack. "I could use a little extra cash," I said, and slid the triangle into place. "Ball in hand, bank the eight?" I asked.

"Ah, shit. Are you serious? I'm finally up a few Benjamins. How 'bout we just shoot?"

"What you worried about Clive?"

He paced at the head of the table. He'd never beaten me. Not once in the past year since I returned to Omaha. I like to believe it's because he learned from his brother, Detrick, who basically sucks, but thinks he's a shooter. Detrick does two things well: organizing Katrina's street crews and killing. Katrina runs Omaha's drug trade. He was her lieutenant. Clive managed to get out of that life and now handles art forgeries. I think of it as a step forward for a kid who came from nothing and is the only member of his family to graduate from high school. And he did it with honors. Once in a while, he helps me out by getting information from people with whom I'd rather not speak.

"All right, let's just play, but don't tell Eddy. He wanted me to take all your money."

"Damn, that's just wrong."

Clive broke, sending the eight ball flying. Then it dropped.

"Shit."

"Yeah, that would've been a few twenties right there. You made the right call. Rack 'em."

We played a few games, and I was feeling a lot more relaxed. My head was clearer, and I was confident that I was right about how Savannah was killed. Now I just needed to find the asshole. I lay my stick onto the table and thanked Clive for the games.

"Anytime, Ms. D. You know, as long as we ain't playing for money."

"Right, Clive." I grabbed my bag and headed for the entrance but stopped at the bar before leaving. Eddy was cleaning up the far end.

"See ya later, Eddy."

He motioned for me to wait while he finished cleaning up. Then he walked over.

"I've been thinking about your problem. It seems to me that I know a guy who might be able to shed some light on that autopsy report."

"Who?"

"This guy worked in the coroner's office around the time Savannah died. Name's Barnes. Shep Barnes."

"Thanks, Eddy."

He waved me off. "I'm sure he's retired by now. I haven't spoken to him in years, so he might not remember me. Used to live on the northwest side not far from a high school."

"I'll find him."

"I'm sure you will baby girl. I'm sure you will." Someone at the opposite end of the bar shouted to get Eddy's attention. Eddy's brow raised. I knew that look. You don't shout in Eddy's general direction unless you want pain.

"Good luck with that," I said and headed straight for the exit. I didn't really want to witness the dressing down that guy was about to receive. I heard Eddy's booming voice as the door shut behind me.

Back in the "smaller-than-an-old-icebox" rental, I phoned Dalton. My "to do" list for him had grown. He picked up on the first ring, sounding a bit out of breath.

"Are you okay?" I asked.

"Yes, Ms. Jackson. Of course. I was in the copy room when the phone rang, that's all."

The copy room was several feet down the hall from Haithem's office.

"I need you to look into a few things for me."

"Yes, of course. Right away."

I gave him a rundown of what needed to happen and when, then I ended the call. Dalton was a good assistant. A little strange, but dependable and thorough. I understood why Haithem chose him.

LOCATING SHEP BARNES turned out to be much easier than I thought it'd be. His plot was in Forest Lawn Cemetery off of Seventy-ninth and Mormon Bridge Road. Discovering this felt like two steps forward and a giant leap backward. I was playing "Mother may I" with a corpse. According to his obituary, he died in a car accident three years ago, leaving behind a wife and two adult children. I tracked down an address for his wife. She still lived in the Florence neighborhood. I phoned ahead and she agreed to meet with me.

Traveling west on State Street reminded me of a time years ago when some friends and I were out, not doing anything we probably should have been on a cold winter night. My friend's old Charger made it half way up the hill before it got stuck and started sliding back. Before we realized what was happening, the front end swung around, and we were rolling fast down the hill. Somehow, he regained control before reaching the bottom. To this day, that night is near the top of the list of scariest uncontrollable events I ever experienced as a teenager.

Mrs. Barnes' house was near the top on the south side of the street. I pulled into her driveway and grabbed my satchel before getting out. Cement stairs led to a cracked concrete path with rose bushes lining both sides to the front porch. An old iron railing with chipped paint provided little in the way of balance as I reached for it and climbed the final steps to the door. She opened it before I knocked. Mrs. Barnes was a petite woman, probably in her late sixties. Her hair was dyed brown and trimmed short. She wore red-framed glasses.

"You must be Ms. Jackson. Come in." She held the door open, allowing me to pass by her.

I entered a small living room with comfortable furniture. A TV was in one corner but turned off. A couch had been placed in front of a bank of windows that faced the street. I never understood why people put their couches in that position. Having my back to a bunch of windows where I can't see who's coming always seemed like a bad idea. Two recliners were opposite the couch.

"May I get you something to drink? Water, iced tea?"

"No, thank you. I'm good."

"Please, sit down. What's this about?"

I chose one of the recliners and she took a spot on the couch.

"Mrs. Barnes, I'm wondering how much Mr. Barnes talked about his job at the coroner's office?"

"Oh, not excessively. It could be gruesome, you know. Mostly, he kept things to himself."

"But not always?"

"No, not always. When you called asking about your sister, I remembered that was one of those times he wasn't quiet. It really was unusual for him to bring his work home with him, so the times that he did, they sort of stood out."

"What do you remember him saying about my sister's case?"

"He was troubled because the coroner he was working with insisted that the reports be altered, but my husband didn't know why."

"Your husband was a technician, right?"

"Yes, he assisted in the office. One of his responsibilities was transcribing the audio from the autopsy. When he was doing that for your sister's case, he told me that was when the coroner instructed him to make changes to the official paper report."

"Did he say what changes were made?"

She stood and crossed the room to an antique secretary desk, pulled the door down, and removed a small notebook. Turning to me, she said, "He made a few notes that might be helpful to you." She walked over and handed it to me. "Whenever Shep was bothered by something at work, he'd write it down in notebooks. Thankfully, Shep being Shep, he always dated the fronts of them, so I was able to find the one for that particular year."

I flipped through the pages and eventually found one for the date Savannah was killed. There were several notes about what the coroner originally found, including the puncture wound behind her left ear. Shep made a note indicating that the coroner wanted the details about the puncture wound listed as irrelevant and likely caused by the victim's earring. He thought this was ridiculous given the fact that the coroner already had reviewed the toxicology report and knew that the victim was injected with poison. Shep believed the coroner was covering for someone but didn't know who or why.

"Did Mr. Barnes ever talk with you about the case, or did he just keep these journals?"

"This case, yes. He'd never been in a position like this. If he didn't do what the coroner instructed, he believed that he'd lose his job, and we couldn't afford for that to happen. Our kids were attending private schools, and I was just beginning my paralegal studies."

"His notes mention a toxicology report, but I never saw one when I reviewed my sister's file."

"He was told to destroy it and replace it with a more benign one."

"Did he say why?"

"No, he wasn't sure, but." She returned to the desk and removed a file. She searched through a series of papers and then wrote something onto a small Post-It note. "If you get in touch with her, she might be able to give you more information."

"Who is she?"

"Shep went to her for legal counsel when this was happening. She's a former family friend. I don't know what he told her because we never discussed it, but things sort of smoothed over and Shep got a promotion a few months later. She and I lost touch a while ago, but you can tell her I suggested that you speak with her."

"He looked the other way."

"Yes, and ever since then it bothered him. The night he had the accident, he'd been drinking. Too much. He lost control of his car, ran a stop sign, and hit a pole head on."

"I didn't realize."

"It's not something we wanted in his obituary, and fortunately, it wasn't front-page news."

I thanked Mrs. Barnes for the information. Resentment crept up inside me like water on the verge of boiling. I needed to track down Susanne Phillips.

A FEW DAYS PASSED BEFORE I was able to find Susanne Phillips and schedule an appointment. She opened her own practice several years ago in Fremont, NE. I wasn't too keen on driving the thirty minutes it would take to get there, especially since I really needed to work on getting Michelle Mathews to return to Omaha. Taking time away from Keeney's case could jam him up, but Phillips couldn't meet with me any other time this week.

I arrived at her downtown office at ten o'clock. It was in an old brick building at E. Fourth and North Main Streets. The building had clearly been renovated to give it a more modern look, with several picture windows installed at street level and large windows added at the second story. J's Steakhouse occupied the corner spot, with a boutique opposite it. Inside there were two other small businesses. Susanne Phillips' office was on the second floor. A young, twenty-something woman greeted me as I entered the suite.

"Ms. Jackson?"

I nodded.

"Susanne will be right with you. I'll let her know that you're here."

She invited me to sit, but I declined. From Phillips' office I had a great view of Main Street. Fremont, NE, wasn't a large community, about twenty-five thousand in town, with roughly another ten thousand in the surrounding area who had Fremont addresses. It had something to do with the Platte River from what I was told the last time I ventured this way.

While I waited, I took in my environment. Phillips' decorating taste was heavily influenced by the Victorian era, with the addition of a hint of Steampunk, which I found fascinating given her age. She had to be around the same age as Mrs. Barnes. I was admiring a clock intermingled with several large and small gears when Ms. Phillips interrupted my focus.

"It's magnificent, isn't it?" she asked.

I turned to see a woman, who I pegged at about five foot seven, wearing a black, pinstriped A-line skirt with a matching fitted vest. To complement the vest and skirt, she wore a long-sleeved white blouse, the collar of which extended up her neck and was accented with small ruffles. The effect was stunning.

"Yes, it's captivating."

"It's a Steampunk arrangement. I'm so glad something finally caught up with my style!" She gestured toward a door to the right of her receptionist's desk.

"Let's go into my office." I followed her into a space outfitted with a mahogany desk and leather high-back chairs. Two for guests, and one for her behind the desk. A large matching bookcase lined the wall behind her desk.

"Please," she said, motioning to one of the guest chairs. "You mentioned something about Shep Barnes when you contacted Jessica. What's this about?" She sat behind her desk, a legal pad in front of her and a pen at the ready.

"I'm not one for games, so I'm just going to be straight with you, so we don't waste any time."

"Please do. I prefer the direct approach, myself."

"Shep Barnes sought legal counsel from you regarding my sister, Savannah's, murder. He was told to dispose of, ignore, or hide evidence. What did you advise him to do?

She set her pen on the desk and sat back in her chair, steepling her hands.

"Ms. Phillips, my family deserves to know the truth."

Her hands fell to the armrests. "You're right. Of course, you're right. But..."

"What?"

"Things were different then. They were struggling financially, and I knew that what I would have advised could really hurt them, so I told Shep what he needed to hear."

"But not what was right."

She looked away for a second, and then she refocused on me. "I told him what I knew would serve his family best."

"And screw mine."

She returned to steepling. "What would you have done?"

I stood, and said, "The right thing."

I left Phillips' office with the understanding that Shep Barnes knew my sister was poisoned, but destroyed the evidence, and now I'd never know who killed her. I'd never know what poison was used so I could execute a search for similar cases. I'd never face Savannah's killer, eye-to-eye, and be able to get justice for my family. I wanted more than justice, but now, I was robbed of that opportunity. And I'd just wasted more than an hour of my friggin day.

Back on the street, I called Dalton and explained what I knew, so far.

"Ms. Jackson, I had no idea. I'll start looking into this right away. You can count on me."

"I appreciate your help, Dalton. I know that this is outside of your duties. I just don't know what direction to go with the limited amount of information I have."

"But, Ms. Jackson, that's not the case."

"What do you mean?" I asked as I unlocked the door to the rental car, tossed my satchel across to the passenger-seat floor, and got inside. I adjusted the driver's side mirror. Someone must have bumped it. Even I felt cramped in the damn car and I'm barely five two.

"You have prints from the knife. True, they probably don't belong to the killer, but they do belong to someone."

Dalton was right. The killer could have intentionally placed another person's prints on the knife. If I found that person, I might be able to find something more useful.

"Dalton, you're a genius!"

"That's why they pay me the big bucks," he said, with a hint of humor in his tone.

He was right; Tracer paid Dalton incredibly well for his assistant position. He'd shown an amazing aptitude for solving complex puzzles, regardless of type.

He could code, too. He was as odd as he was charming. Endearing even.

"Let me know what you find."

"I'm on it, Ms. Jackson, don't you worry."

The line disconnected and I was feeling much better. Almost elated. Okay, not quite, but a hell of a lot better than when I was sitting in Phillips' office.

I started the engine of my tiny rental, longing for the view from the driver's seat of my Jeep and headed back to Omaha. By the time I got there, my stomach was rumbling. I'd driven in on West Maple Road and had plenty of food options, but I knew exactly what I needed – pizza. I'd heard about a pizza joint that used fresh mozzarella and I had to try it. So, once I hit 144th Street, I jogged north to Fort Street and then a few blocks east to 142nd Street.

Pizzeria Davlo was in a strip mall, with a bunch of businesses I'd never heard of, mainly because I don't usually get this far northwest. When it comes to pizza, I'm strictly a New-York-style woman, so when I entered and discovered that theirs was Chicago style I was about to turn back, but then the owner showed me what they offered, and a cracker crust – my second preferred style - was on their menu. As I waited at the bar for my order to arrive, I enjoyed a glass of Merlot. My mouth watered at the mere thought of sinking my teeth into the Spicy Hawaiian slices. When the pizza was placed in front of me the aroma floated to my nose. I inhaled deeply and sighed. This was going to be mind-altering.

FEELING GUILTY ABOUT not making forward progress on Keeney's case the last few days, I contacted Michael to ask if he'd spoken with his sister. He had, but so far, she didn't have plans to return to Omaha. This got me more curious about her. Why wouldn't she come back? Was it her relationship with Bridgeton? And then it hit me. What if she started seeing him again after Sarah was murdered? Or what if she never stopped? It was time to dig a little deeper into Michelle's past if I was going to either rule her in as a potential suspect, or out.

Charlie answered on the first ring.

"LaRoche Investigations," he said with his baritone voice.

"Charlie, Dez. I need another favor."

"More than I'm already doing? You might have to start paying for my services," he joked. He would never send me a bill. Trading, working together, and finding connections was more his style.

"See if you can find out how long Michelle Mathews has been in New Orleans and if she left at any point. Also find out where she went, who she might have met—the usual."

"You still trying to make connections with her to your guys in Omaha?"

"Not exactly. I know she was connected to both of them. What I don't know is if she's still in touch with one of them, or if the relationship ended."

"What's the case you're working, anyway?"

I filled him in on the high points, leaving out the details that he didn't need for the task at hand.

"The vic's twin sister? Ain't that some messed up shit? So, what are you thinking, she did the deed?"

"That's one angle. It wouldn't be the first time someone killed a family member out of jealousy or rage. From what Sam Myers told me, Michelle isn't completely stable. Her own brother admitted that she hasn't handled her sister's death well. Hearsay, I know, but words of caution just the same."

"No doubt. Okay, I'll see what I can turn up here and holler back when I have something you can run with."

After hanging up with Charlie, I decided to take my chances and see if I could meet with Cal Bridgeton. It was time for a "come to Jesus" meeting. When I arrived at the offices of Bridgeton & Myers, two police cars were parked in the lot. Media crews were setting up cameras while reporters primped. From my vehicle,

I saw Cal Bridgeton being led out by two detectives. Reporters swarmed. The detectives waved them back and the officers blocked their advance on Bridgeton. I lowered my window so that I might be able to hear what was being said. Bridgeton's head was erect, shoulders back. Even cuffed he walked with confidence.

"This is a mistake," I heard him say in response to a reporter's query. "This will all be cleared up by the end of the day, I assure you."

Sam Myers stood in the entrance to the building, hands in his pockets, and shoulders slightly hunched as if he were cold. It was a warm day. Warmer than usual as a matter of fact. Reporters approached him, but he returned inside the building without saying anything. I waited for Bridgeton to be escorted away and the media to pack up before heading inside to find out what happened.

Staff members spoke in hushed tones throughout the entryway as I made my way to the elevator. The doors opened and I entered, followed by Daniel. The exact person I wanted to see right now.

"I just can't believe it."

I turned to face him. "What happened?"

"They accused Mr. Bridgeton of murder."

"What? Who?"

"I don't know. They didn't say, but it was a woman. Someone overheard one of the officers say that it was some engineer. She works downtown."

"Seriously?"

He nodded. "And Mr. Myers is playing it cool as a cucumber, but I know he's got to be completely panicked."

"More than what you'd expect?"

"Yes. They were meeting with another firm, today. The big wigs were in the conference room when the detectives arrived."

"What was the deal supposed to be about?"

"They planned to partner on some major project. It would mean a lot of exposure and, of course, money for the firm."

"Well, if exposure is what they wanted, they're about to get a pretty healthy dose now."

Daniel exited the elevator, but I didn't follow. There wasn't any point in talking with Sam Myers right now. What I wanted to know most was who the woman was, so I returned to my car, and started googling on my phone. Sure enough, it was already hitting news outlets. The woman was Kristy Briggs.

Shocked, I phoned a contact I had at the downtown Omaha Police Department. Officer Jacobs picked up on the third ring.

"Hi, Officer Jacobs. This is Dezeray Jackson."

There was an audible sigh, and then he asked, "Yes, Ms. Jackson. How may I help you? Is something on fire, or has someone been shot in front of you, lately?" We had a bit of a history. He was the first to arrive at my house early last year when someone set my front door ablaze. A month or so after that, Godfrey discovered a severed hand in my back yard. And then a few months ago, he and his partner were the first on the scene when a guy I knew as Alec Covington was shot by a sniper.

"Well, now that you mention it, I was wondering if you could tell me if Cal Bridgeton was brought downtown."

"What do you have to do with Cal Bridgeton?"

"Nothing. Not exactly, anyway."

"Then why are you trying to get information?"

Officer Jacobs really should have been a detective a long time ago. I had no idea why he wasn't.

"He's connected to a case I'm working, and I might actually be able to provide some useful info to the detectives on the case."

"In exchange for?"

"I just need to ask him a few questions."

"It's not gonna happen. You know we have procedures to follow."

"What if I spoke to the detectives and told them what I needed to know. Would they tell me what he said?"

"This is an active, ongoing investigation, Ms. Jackson. If you have information that is pertinent to it, please come down to the precinct. Otherwise, if there's nothing more, I need to get back to the pile of reports I was working on."

Damn. I was really hoping I'd developed a better rapport with him.

BEING STRUCK DOWN BY Officer Jacobs was discouraging, but not fatal. I did happen to know a reporter at The Omaha World-Herald who might be able to help me out. I called Cynthia Cruz and we agreed to meet at Jimmy John's on Fourteenth and Farnam Streets to grab sandwiches. When I walked into the shop, Cynthia was at the counter ordering. I waited near the fountain drinks.

"I ordered you tuna, barbecue chips and a Coke." She handed me a cup.

"Thanks."

I met Cynthia a few months after I relocated to Omaha. She'd attended a women's self-defense class I was teaching at my gym. In my line of work, it's usually helpful to know a reporter or two, especially if they handle the crime beat. That was what motivated Cynthia to take the seminar. I don't teach often, but through the course of the class, she and I became friends, and we meet once a week to train. She doesn't want to learn a particular style. She just wants to be able to handle herself if she finds herself in a scary situation. I encouraged her to get a gun permit, but she wasn't having any of that.

We took our food outside and sat at one of Jimmy John's tables. Before Omaha, I'd never experienced their freaky-fast service. So far, I'd had every sandwich on their menu at least once. I opened my bag of chips, first, then had to tap the Coke.

"What do you want to know about Cal Bridgeton?"

"Look, this is just between the two of us."

"Of course," she said, and took a bite of her Club sandwich. She always ordered the same thing and never drank soda.

"Do you remember Michelle Mathews?"

"Michael Mathews' daughter?"

I nodded. "I'm investigating her sister's murder."

"But that was solved. The police charged a guy named James Keeney. I covered that story."

"I know, and that's who I'm working for. I have reason to believe that he didn't have anything to do with Sarah Bridgeton's death."

Cynthia set her sandwich back on the table, and sipped her iced tea, while her eyebrows raised, encouraging me to keep talking.

"How much do you know about Cal Bridgeton?" I asked.

"Same as everyone else, I suppose."

"And what about the woman he's accused of murdering?"

"So far, I know about her work history, but not much about her private life. Why? What do you know?"

"Kristy Briggs and Bridgeton did have a relationship."

"And by "relationship" you mean?"

"They were sexual partners."

"An affair, then."

"No, just sex. Apparently, they're both addicts."

Cynthia had been drinking her tea when I announced that. She nearly sprayed it all over the table and me.

"Oh, my God. This is good."

"It gets better."

"Really? Go on." She started eating her sandwich again, while listening intently.

"I was trying to find potential suspects—other people who could've killed Sarah, besides Keeney."

"And you thought Bridgeton?"

I nodded. "But now that doesn't make as much sense, since he's been arrested for killing Briggs."

"It makes perfect sense."

"How so?" I asked.

"Maybe it was an accident. You know, some sex act gone bad sort of thing."

"Do you know how Briggs was killed?" I asked.

"My sources told me that she was strangled, so it's possible."

"Yeah, but not probable. Briggs told me she and Bridgeton were taking a break because he was pursuing another woman. Someone in his office. And there's also Michelle."

"What about Michelle?"

"That's who Bridgeton did have an affair with."

Cynthia was mid bite when she dropped her sandwich. "Holy shit! You're lying to me."

I shook my head.

"These are some twisted rich people."

"Uh, huh."

"So, what is it you need me to do? I mean, I get the feeling there's something else."

"I need you to ask Bridgeton a few questions about his relationship with Michelle. His lawyer is going to bond him out, there's no question about that. But he's not going to talk to me. I sort of burned that bridge."

She fished her phone from her purse, removed the stylus and said, "Shoot."

"Sarah Bridgeton kept a diary. See if Bridgeton knew about it."

"Uh, huh." She started writing.

"I'm betting that he did. The diary is how I found out about his relationship with Michelle. Ask him when he met Michelle."

She looked up from her phone. "Do you think they knew each other before he married her sister?"

"I don't know, but I need to figure out when they met and how things started between them."

"Anything else?"

"Michelle was involved with his partner, Sam Myers. See if you can figure out what Bridgeton thought about their relationship. Right now, all I have to go on is what Myers told me."

"What was that?"

"Bridgeton is a competitive man and when he wants something, he gets it. Basically. Something along those lines, anyway."

"Have you tried talking to Michelle?"

"I'm working on that. She was MIA for a while, but I know where she is now."

"What about their brother?"

"I've met with him a few times, but he doesn't seem to know about Michelle and Bridgeton's relationship."

She set her phone on the table. "Okay, as soon as he's released, I'll see if I can get a meeting. His lawyers won't want him talking about Briggs, but they might not see any harm in this line of questions."

"They're lawyers, Cynthia. They'll have an issue with all of it, so you're going to have to play this from a different angle."

"Any ideas where he likes to frequent?"

"A few, yeah." I gave Cynthia a short list of places I knew she could find Bridgeton and would have an opportunity to get to know him better. She was a beautiful Latina, and I had a feeling Bridgeton wouldn't be able to resist, even if he knew who she was.

Cynthia checked the time. "Oh, shoot! I need to get going. There's a press conference for that gang killing that happened a few months back. You remember?"

"The bodies on the tracks?"

"Yep. Gruesome stuff. Absolutely horrible."

"What's the press conference about?"

"Rumor is, the police arrested someone."

"Who"

"Detrick, "Mad Dog," Dixon."

That was the kind of news I liked hearing. Mad Dog had never been caught or connected to any of his crimes, before. It looked like it was time for him to pay the piper, as the saying goes. Then Clive flashed into my mind. Detrick was his brother, after all, and him finally going to prison could dramatically change Clive's circumstances. I made a mental note to track Clive down before the end of the day.

CHAPTER SEVEN

AFTER LEAVING CYNTHIA, I had a change of plans. I wanted to backtrack and talk with Sam Myers, but it didn't make sense to drive west, then come back east to find Clive, later. I'd probably have better luck tracking him down now, anyway. His brother, Detrick, owned an old warehouse building in North Omaha and Clive ran his art business from there. I decided to take Twenty-fourth Street and reminisce. My family didn't live in that part of North Omaha when I was a kid, but we visited about every other week to get barbecue.

A lot had changed since I was gone. New buildings popped up and eager, enthusiastic entrepreneurs filled the spaces. Houses replaced old low-income housing projects. And from what I heard recently, there'd be more development in the near future. There was still the problem of not enough jobs, and too many gang members roaming the streets and neighborhoods, but things were moving in the right direction.

I drove east at Locust Street and parked across from the large brick building. The door was ajar when I approached, so I stopped outside and listened. Satisfied that nothing, or no one would jump out at me when I entered, I pulled the door open wider and stepped into the hall. I followed it into a large open space with high ceilings and exposed pipes. This wasn't my first visit to Clive's office, but it had been a while. He still had a metal desk with chipped paint, a wood chair, and an overstuffed, used couch. It all looked odd sitting at the far end of such an expansive space.

I didn't pry into Clive's business. What I didn't know, I didn't feel obligated to report to the police. And he was just a kid trying to make it in a family of drug dealers. The fact that Detrick made sure to push Clive out was the only positive thing that I could say about Mad Dog. He was a hard, dangerous, manipulative, smooth-talking son of a bitch who I'd love to see put away for the rest of his life. The only people I felt sorry for in his life were his kids. He had ten last I heard. Clive was sitting at his desk talking on his phone when he noticed me come into the room. He started talking faster and finished his call.

"Ms. D? What brings you this far east?" He leaned back in his chair, stretching his hands behind his head.

"Do you know about Detrick?"

He sat up straighter and said, "Yeah, I heard."

"What's your plan if he goes down?"

"I got it covered, don't worry."

"Clive, he's protected you from a lot of people, some of your own family, even."

"I know, but I got me a pretty good thing going with the art. My other brothers won't mess with it. Detrick runs the show, no matter what happens."

"In my experience, when the big dog gets put down, another one takes his place."

"I ain't got other options."

"There might be one."

"Oh, yeah, what's that?"

"You could work for me." The words flew out of my mouth before my head caught up.

"Doing what?"

"Legwork. Basic research."

"Ah, man. I can't work for you."

"Why not?"

"Do you honestly think me working for you is gonna stop Katrina forcing me back into the life?"

"She won't. I'll talk with her."

"You're probably the only one besides Detrick who can."

"You're interested, then?"

"Only if Detrick goes down. Like I said, this art thing is working well for me."

"You'd have to step away from it if you work for me. I can't have full knowledge of what you're doing and then fail to report it."

Clive was still young enough to mold. If he got out of this and was surrounded by high achievers making good money, he'd rise to their level. He proved he had it in him during high school.

"Clive?"

"Yeah, yeah. I got it."

"All right, I'm out. I've got leads to follow." I handed him my card. "Get in touch as soon as you hear anything indicating Detrick is being replaced."

"If it happens, where am I supposed to go? I been staying with him."

"We'll figure that out when the time comes. For now, have a bag packed and be ready to bolt."

"Why are you doin' this for me?"

"Because, Clive, you're not an idiot like the rest of them and you deserve a chance. Besides, if my Great Aunt Violet was alive, she'd kick my ass if I didn't step up. You might not remember her, but she was hell to handle when she got pissed. Ask Detrick sometime. He knew her." Of course, if she were still alive, I wouldn't be in Omaha, but that wasn't important to point out.

When I left Clive I was feeling good about how things might play out. Katrina owed me a favor, so I was confident that I could get her to ensure that her crew stayed away from Clive. And if I was going to be completely honest, it would be nice to have my own assistant. Dalton was great, but he worked for Haithem, and he wasn't street-level leg work material. I could train Clive. If things did go south for Detrick, I'd get Clive set up in one of Tracer's safe houses for a while until the dust settled and the killing stopped. I knew from years working drug cases in Miami that a changing of the guard always involved bloodshed. As long as I could keep Clive out of the middle of things, I'd be satisfied.

Normally, I'd go to Katrina's club to talk with her, but I decided to call, instead. She was still on my shit list and seeing her might trigger a negative physical response that I wouldn't feel compelled to stop. If anyone deserved a beatdown, it was Katrina. She was Detrick in a dress and stilettos, with an even keener sense for manipulation. It wasn't a surprise that he was her right hand. She answered by the second ring.

"Are they your lawyers or Detrick's?" I asked.

"Dez, you haven't forgiven me, I take it?" When I didn't respond, she said, "Mine."

Strike one for OPD. Katrina had amazingly resourceful and talented lawyers on her payroll. They were the reason charges were never brought against her for dealing.

"What do you think will happen?"

"That's not for me to say, but if you're asking if I believe Detrick will serve even one day at The Pen, then my answer is 'no.'"

"I appreciate your confidence, but I like to plan."

"What does any of this have to do with you?"

"Clive."

"Ah, I see. You're worried that he'll be brought back into the family trade."

"He's going to be working for me."

"Really? That's a novel idea."

"You don't need him, Katrina."

"My business always needs young men like Clive. They're a remarkable sales force. Highly motivated."

She was messing with me, which is exactly why we weren't speaking in person. There was a time when she and I were friends, but she decided to go a different direction. Some would say we're still friends but estranged. As much as she pisses me off, I knew she would always have my back, and some part of me would never turn away from her, either.

"He's going to give up the art business, too."

"Well, now, you're not doing anything to convince me that I should allow him to go. Do you have any idea how much of that art venture I own?"

"I don't want to know."

"Here's the deal. Unlike Detrick, you have nothing to trade. In some form or another, I've taken care of Clive Dixon his entire existence. A piece of his art business was Detrick's offer in return for getting Clive off the streets."

"How about I don't give you a much deserved beatdown? That seems like a good deal."

"We both know that you don't mean that."

"Do we?"

"You should be more careful, Dez. I know everything there is to know about you."

"Not everything. Clive Dixon is off limits."

I could sense that she was smiling.

"Dez, all you had to do was ask nicely. Threats aren't necessary."

I disconnected and tossed my phone onto the passenger seat. Katrina was my best friend during high school. When we met our freshman year, she was dating a real asshole. I taught her how to fire a gun and break a person's wrists and fingers. One night the three of us went to a local burger joint. He tried to smack her when he thought she was looking at another guy. She blocked him with her left hand, got a hold of his wrist and applied a lock I'd recently shown her. He hit the ground hard. Even now, the memory of seeing him go down so fast makes me smile. Katrina was around when I dated Patrick Murphy. She was there the day he joined the Marines, and I was so pissed that I wouldn't say goodbye. I was angry that she threw her life down the shitter for a quick buck.

STILL ANNOYED BY MY conversation with Katrina, I opted to channel my negative energy into something more positive and drove to Bridgeton & Myers. I'd phoned ahead and Myers agreed to meet with me to talk about what happened in the morning. I was surprised because I'd assumed that he would clam up, too afraid to cause damage to either their business or Bridgeton's reputation.

I knocked on the door to Myers' office. He was seated at his desk reviewing a pile of papers. He invited me to sit.

"Can you believe this?" He shuffled through the papers. "Our PR firm sent all of this to me so that we can begin to manage the situation."

"Wow. That was quick."

"Not quick enough. I've already been contacted by every media outlet in Omaha, plus a few in Lincoln. This is ridiculous." He shoved the papers aside. "I don't know what the hell he could have been thinking."

"Are we talking about Mr. Bridgeton?"

"Yes." He stared at me as if I should have known.

"You're assuming that he's guilty."

"You've done your investigating. You know what type of man he is. They found her strangled, for Christ's sake."

"That doesn't mean that he killed her." I couldn't believe I'd taken this position, but since I did, I planned to let it play out.

"He's got a fetish for that sort of thing."

"How do you know that?"

"I've known him since college. He'd brag about his sexual prowess and what the girls would let him do to them. He was proud of it."

"Still, that isn't proof."

"Maybe not, but this might be." He reached into his bottom-right desk drawer, pulled out a file, and handed it to me. "If the police see this. Shit. I don't know what I should do. It's not as if partners have some sort of privilege like a spouse. We should, dammit."

"What is this, exactly?"

"Cal was taking pictures of their meetings."

"Why'd he give them to you?"

"For the same reason that he always told me about his escapades during college."

I flipped through the photos and sure enough, there were images of him strangling her.

"Is this everything?"

"Yes, thankfully."

"Do you really believe that he could have done this?"

He absentmindedly unfolded a paper clip.

"I don't know, maybe. And if he did this, then maybe he killed Sarah, too. Oh, my God. This is horrible." He dropped the paper clip, stood, and paced behind his desk. His right hand stroked his head.

"You might be jumping ahead here."

"That night, he was seeing Ms. Briggs, but what if when he got home, Sarah confronted him?"

"What makes you think she would?"

"She knew about his affairs."

"How do you know that?"

"I mean, she had to know about his affairs. How couldn't she? Sarah was an intelligent woman."

"I can't tell you how many times I've seen someone blindsided by a cheating spouse."

"Should I show these to the police?"

"I'm not an attorney, Mr. Myers, so I can't help you with this. What I can tell you is that I don't believe Mr. Bridgeton killed Sarah. I think he's too caught up in himself to have done it. Think about it, he had a beautiful wife, who by all accounts, loved him, and he was able to sleep with other women. What man would want to ruin a sweet deal like that?"

I didn't completely buy what I was feeding him, but I also found it strange that he was so quick to assume that Bridgeton was capable of murder. Yes, some people really are, but most people aren't, even when pushed. Why would Myers need to believe Bridgeton was guilty? How would that help him?

"Mr. Myers, call your attorney," I said, and stood to leave. "Your PR people can't handle this for you, no matter how good they are."

I left still feeling perplexed by the interaction. I got the distinct impression that Myers didn't like his partner. But why start a business with someone you hate?

RUSH-HOUR TRAFFIC WAS just getting into full swing by the time I left Bridgeton & Myers' office. Luckily, I was headed east. Rather than go straight home, like I knew I should so that I could check on Godfrey, and catch up on client emails uninterrupted, my little rental pointed me in the direction of Brazen Head Irish Pub off of Seventy-eighth and Dodge Streets. As I entered the lot, I realized that I wasn't the only one who decided they needed a Guinness. I left my satchel in the car so I wouldn't be tempted to deal with emails while enjoying a pint. I learned a longtime ago not to answer emails while drinking, no matter if it was one drink, or more.

A decent-sized crowd of young professionals occupied the wood tables throughout the front of the restaurant, while a few more mingled at the bar. One of my favorite things about Brazen Head is the bar. The entire thing was built in Ireland and modeled after the oldest pub in Dublin, also named Brazen Head. I found a spot on the far side, ordered my beer and a Brian Boru Boxty. It was basically a potato pancake filled with Irish sausage, champ potatoes and cheddar cheese. You can never have too many potatoes in my opinion.

By around six o'clock the crowd increased. I'd finished my food and ordered another beer when the spot next to me finally opened up, giving me some much-needed elbow room. Then, some guy sat down. He gave me a little nod and smiled. The bartender took his order: a shot with a beer chaser, and by the looks of it, this wasn't his first round.

"Name's Tom," he said, a bit slower than I'm sure he realized. Under normal circumstances I would have made a quick exit, but I'd just ordered my beer.

"Dez," I said, and moved my chair away slightly, pushing into a few people who were standing near me. "Sorry." This being Nebraska, the offended shook it off.

Several minutes of silence passed before Tom struck up a conversation.

"Why do women always go for the other guy?" He turned to face me. His cheeks had the rosy sheen of someone who couldn't handle his liquor but tried his best to hide that fact.

"Excuse me?" I asked.

"Women. You're a woman." He knocked back the shot, slammed the glass down, and took a pull from his beer. "What's wrong with going for the nice guy once in a while? I mean, look at me, I'm a good-looking guy. I've got a respectable, well-paying job." He burped. "Sorry."

I covered my nose with my napkin, pretending to wipe my mouth. He started again. "She's going back to him even though she knows he's an asshole. She knows."

He smacked his hand onto the bar for emphasis. I sat back in my chair, crossing my arms in front of my chest. No one around us was paying any attention to this obviously inebriated guy.

"Would you do that?" he slurred.

"It's probably the sex."

His eyes opened wider, and he leaned toward me. "I'm great in bed."

"I'm sure you are."

"No, really. I studied the Kama Sutra and shit." He reached for his beer. "I did it for her. I'm not into all that, but seriously, we had great sex." He raised a finger in the air, signaling the bartender.

I was about to finish my beer when the bartender gave me a refill. Apparently, it was a gift from my new intoxicated friend.

"I'm just trying to understand. You think I'm good-looking, right?"

"Sure," I said.

"I don't know what she sees in him. I've known him for years. He's a real dick." He finished his beer and started on his second. "I can say that 'cause we're friends. I mean, I know he's a dick to women. Always has been. Ever since high school. That's how long we've known each other."

"That's a long time."

"Yeah, it is."

There was a short pause, and then a tall, blond-haired guy dressed in a tailored suit, blue striped tie, and with a dazzling smile, stepped up behind Tom.

He put his hands on his shoulders.

"Ah, my friend, Tom, here, isn't causing you too much trouble, I hope?"

"Nope, we were just chatting."

Tom looked sideways at his friend.

"I was just telling her about you," Tom said.

"All good?"

Tom didn't answer. I flashed a not-so-sincere smile.

"I'm Rick." He offered his hand.

"Dez, and I was just leaving. You can have my seat."

"But you haven't finished your beer," Tom said.

"Thanks for that, but my dog is waiting for me at home. If I leave him too long, there will be hell to pay." I slid the beer closer to him.

"Maybe I'll see you again, sometime," Tom said.

"I doubt it." I left money for my tab, stood, and maneuvered between a few people before escaping through the front door.

Inside the safety of my rental car, I checked messages. There was only one and relief swept over me. My Jeep was finally ready, and I could pick it up in the morning. I started the car and drove home, thinking about my new friend, Tom. Here he was complaining about the very guy he was at Brazen Head with, and they were still friends. It reminded me of my clearly messed up relationship with Katrina, but it also reminded me of another relationship—Bridgeton and Myers.

What makes us stay around the people who piss us off the most? Why do we insist on hanging on? In my case, I could walk away from Katrina, never looking back. I did it before when I left Omaha the first time. Now that I'd returned, why couldn't I keep clear of her? And what about Myers? After college, he made a decision to partner with Bridgeton. Who goes into business with a person he loathes? I was still thinking about this when I pulled into my driveway.

I could hear Godfrey on the other side of the door, whining. I'd made him wait too long and his bladder was probably ready to explode. As soon as I opened the door, he darted out. When he finished, he barreled past me and straight into the kitchen. He was definitely feeling better. I'd picked up a treat for him from Brazen Head. He danced around and around as I unwrapped his burger.

"I hope your tummy can handle this." He'd started drooling and sort of hopping up and down. I split the burger in half and handed him a piece. One gulp and it was gone. "You could chew it first, Godfrey." I handed him the other half.

I'd had enough crap for the day and decided to watch *Arrow* on Netflix, enjoy a glass of wine, and snack on popcorn. I sprinkled it with a cheese powder, and glass in hand, settled down in my oversize chair in the living room, and put my feet up. Godfrey joined me and climbed up onto the couch. I'd given up trying to get him to stay off of it about a month after I brought him home from the shelter. My wine to the right and the bowl in my lap, I turned on the TV. Then my phone rang.

"Dalton? What is it?"

"You received a package today. Do you want me to open it?"

"Does it say who it's from?"

"No."

"All right, then. Set it on my desk. I'll be in Lincoln tomorrow. Anything else?"

"I forwarded a few inquiries to you. You'll need to review them and let me know who's assigned to follow up. I was able to find more information about Michelle Mathews."

That got my attention. I hadn't asked Dalton to continue searching because I'd contacted Charlie.

"What did you find?"

"It would seem that Ms. Mathews left Omaha shortly after her sister's murder. She didn't attend the funeral. Her next stop was Cannes, France, where she remained for several months. Mr. Mathews told you that she went to Buenos Aires sometime last year, right?"

"Yes, why?"

"It looks like she was just passing through. The information I have is that she was in Cannes and then returned to the states. That's why I picked up a trail in New York City. She left and returned to Cannes. I think she went to Buenos Aires to meet her brother."

"Maybe she didn't want him to know about Cannes for some reason."

"That's what I was thinking." There was a brief pause, and then, "There's something else."

"What?"

"Identical twins don't have the same fingerprints."

"So."

"I wasn't sure if you were aware of that."

"Dalton, Tracer should pay you more!"

THE NEXT MORNING, I called Dawn Ryker at The Lab. I wanted her to review everything we had about the Bridgeton crime scene. I didn't expect an immediate answer to what I suspected, so I grabbed my satchel and returned the rental car. Getting my Jeep back was my number-one priority. The mechanic didn't tell me anything I didn't already know from what Murphy said when he examined the car. Cut wires can lead to a nasty case of the crispies.

I loved everything about my black Jeep Cherokee. It was roomy enough to accommodate Godfrey, all my training equipment, and during a surveillance gig, it was comfortable. I kept a plug-in cooler in the front, on the passenger-side floor. It held all the essentials. I didn't always have the luxury of hitting a drive-thru while watching someone. The cooler was one of the best purchases I made while living in Miami. I hate Miami. Damn. Even the thought of it put me in a bad mood.

The drive to Lincoln passed quickly because I'd started listening to audio books. I couldn't listen to fiction because it would put me to sleep, so I listened to self-improvement, business, and investing books. Once in a while, I'd find a podcast I liked and would binge-listen to past episodes. A radio drama called *Adventure Frequency* kept my attention on longer drives. Fiction, I know, but action-packed and with voice actors playing different roles.

I parked in Haithem's old spot and entered Tracer International from the back. A security station at every point of entry to the building greeted visitors. I placed my satchel, guns, and knives onto the belt for scanning and walked through the detector. When they were initially installed, I'd conceal a weapon just to test them. The guards didn't appreciate it because it meant more paperwork for them. Rick greeted me and handed my satchel back, after I took my weapons.

"You use those knives much?" he asked.

"Only when absolutely necessary."

"When was the last time it was necessary?"

"A couple months back." I smiled and entered the elevator.

Dalton waited for me outside the elevator door with a bottle of Coke. He handed it to me and began briefing me on the day's activities. Apparently, I had one or two meetings to attend. Times like this made me wish Haithem would return sooner rather than later. He was much better at sitting patiently through executive meetings.

"I left the box in your office." He didn't follow me inside.

The box contained more pictures of activities at Abaci Transportation Corporation. There weren't any notes on the pictures explaining what I was supposed to be looking for, but Haithem did include a Post-It note with a series of numbers on it. My guess was that it was a safe code, but I didn't know where he had a safe. I put everything back inside the box and closed it. Then I went to find Dalton and located him a few minutes later in the copy room talking with another assistant. He saw me, ended his conversation, and followed me back to Haithem's office.

"Does Haithem have a safe in this office?"

"Yes, of course. Two, in fact."

"Do you know the codes?"

"No."

"Where are they?"

"One is behind that picture to the right," he was pointing behind the desk. "And the other one is inside that table." He pointed to the ornately carved wood table from Morocco.

I thanked Dalton and he left, closing the door behind him. I tried the wall safe first but guessed wrong. Then I tried the other one. Still wrong. What the hell? Then it occurred to me that he probably had a safe in his former apartment. Normally, I wouldn't think twice about going to Haithem's place, but for the past several months, it hasn't been his place, anymore. It was given to another director. That was Haithem's official title, though he never used it. Now I'd have to either convince the person to let me search the apartment, or break in. My money was on breaking in.

"Dalton?" I peeked outside the office. "Do you know which director moved into Haithem's apartment?"

"Yes, Ms. Jackson. That would be Steve Cochran, Director of Security."

Shit.

"Anything else, Ms. Jackson?"

"Could you find out where he is right now?"

"Sure. Do you want me to let him know that you'd like to speak with him?"

I stepped out of the office, walked over to Dalton's desk, and said, "No, Dalton. I'd like you to keep this to yourself, please."

He nodded, turned to his computer, and worked his magic. Within seconds, I knew where Cochran was, where he was scheduled to be, and most importantly, that he wasn't at his apartment.

FIGURING I HAD PLENTY of time to search Haithem's old apartment, I left Tracer and walked a few blocks to the building. It was located in the Haymarket area, a section of Lincoln that had seen a resurgence over the past several years. The district runs from "O" Street to the south and "R" Street to the north, and from Ninth Street on the east side to Canopy Street to the west. During summer months it's host to a large Saturday morning farmers market and bustles with people from throughout the city. Other times, you're more likely to find businesspeople enjoying the local restaurants and coffee shops, along with students from the University of Nebraska-Lincoln.

Haithem's building had a secured door, but the entry code remained the same as when he lived there. At this time of the day, I didn't expect to see many residents coming and going. I entered the empty elevator and rode it to the top. I liked his apartment more than the one I was provided while living in Miami, but then I liked just about everything more than anything I experienced in Miami. That was five years of hell.

The door locks had been changed, so I picked them, which didn't prove challenging. I was surprised that Cochran didn't insist on something more secure, especially given the supposed circumstances surrounding Haithem's demise. I entered a small entryway and quietly closed the door behind me. My plan was simple—go room to room until I located the safe. Time was on my side and that was a welcome change of pace.

Tracer apartments came fully furnished and included all the latest tech, but employees usually added some of their own style. So far, what I gleaned from the living, dining and kitchen areas was that Cochran wasn't into decorating. The apartments didn't usually include an installed safe, so Haithem must have either bought one, and hid it, or had one added. If it were me, I would hide one, but Haithem probably didn't do that. He'd been stationary in recent years.

I began my search by checking the more obvious locations-behind pictures and wall hangings. There were maybe ten throughout the entire space. When I didn't find the safe, I moved to the less obvious places beneath a floorboard, behind the refrigerator, behind one of the two TVs—places like that. I was really hoping I wasn't going to need to remove the TVs from the walls. I'm strong, but short, and maneuvering them without them tumbling to the floor would be difficult.

Back in the kitchen, I looked through the cabinets for a special compartment. Nothing. Then I wrestled the refrigerator from its spot in a corner. The damn thing was one of those Viking lookalikes. After what seemed like hours, I managed to get it moved enough so that I could look behind it. My effort was rewarded. I spent the next fifteen minutes moving each side of the behemoth back and forth until I could squeeze past the wall and get behind it. The safe was approximately the size of a bread box. I entered the code, heard a click, and the door popped open. The inside wasn't deeper than the length of my forearm. Haithem had several papers, a few passports, and money in the safe. I gathered it up, closed the safe, and slid out of my cell.

"What the hell are you doing here?" Steve Cochran stood in the center of the kitchen; arms crossed staring me down. He was an imposing man at about six five, and stalwart.

"Um," I wasn't sure what to say and a lie hadn't formed in my head as fast as usual. "Nothing." I held the contents of the safe behind my back. "I was just..."

"You have two seconds to tell me what you're doing in my apartment, Jackson."

Normally, I'd be all about lying, but this situation seemed to call for the truth, or at least some version of it.

"Here's the deal,"

"I'm listening." He hadn't budged from his spot.

"I knew Haithem had a safe installed and thought I should grab what was inside before someone else discovered it." I could see by his expression that I'd chosen the right angle to play.

"Why not just ask me?"

"That's a great question."

Arms still folded in front of him, he peered down at me. I took a small step back.

"I know you're a busy man, and it was just as simple for me to come in, grab what I needed, and go."

"You broke in."

"True, but..." I didn't know where else to take this, so I spun it back at him, "What are you doing here, anyway? You're supposed to be at a meeting."

"Let me guess. Your boy, Dalton, told you my schedule. Sometimes schedules change, Jackson. That, and I saw you."

"How?"

He pointed to strategically placed, well-hidden cameras. "There," he said, pointing to a vase filled with flowers. "And there." A picture on an end table.

Shit.

"I brought those along from my other place. You never know who you might see. What'd you find, his cache?"

"Yeah. I'm going to turn it in. It's not a good idea to leave this sort of thing around, ya know? Knowing Haithem as well as I did, I knew he had to have one."

"Yeah, I know. What's in it?"

"Papers, passports, nothing unexpected, but I haven't looked through it, yet."

"Let me see them," he extended his hand expectantly.

"No, that's all right. I'll take care of this."

"I'm director of security, remember? I'm going to see the papers eventually."

That was true – if I'd had any intention of actually turning them in.

"Right, eventually."

"Jackson."

"Cochran."

His hands rested on his hips, and he took a wider stance. He reminded me of the times my father would do this after he caught me sneaking into the house. It never had the desired effect.

After several minutes staring at each other in silence, he said, "Fine. But I want to see them by the end of the day."

"No problem." That gave me plenty of time to review them and make copies. I'd wait for Murphy to get back in touch and I'd get everything to him.

"The passports, too."

Crap. There were four. Cochran didn't know that, so I'd just hand in one.

"You can leave now."

I smiled and headed straight for the door.

"And Jackson, don't let me catch you here, again."

"Will do," I gave him a short, backhanded wave and left. I didn't anticipate ever needing to repeat this, so I wasn't worried.

BY SEVEN O'CLOCK THAT night I was back in Omaha and headed to Eddy's to meet Murphy. I'd stopped at home briefly to check on Godfrey and let him outside.

Since I knew someone was watching me, I brought him back in before leaving. I figured that the creep originally got inside on a day when Godfrey was out.

Whoever he was, he knew about Godfrey and probably would rather not get to know him better, as much as I'd enjoy seeing them meet.

Murphy was in what had become his usual spot at the far end of the bar. I took the seat next to his. Eddy wasn't behind the bar, but someone new was.

"Clive? What are you doing here?" I asked.

"Eddy's teaching me about his business. You know, somethin legit."

That was an interesting comment considering what I knew about Eddy's business. He didn't just own the billiard hall; he dealt in weapons of all kinds. Sometimes they were legal.

"Whatchya havin'?"

I ordered a gin and tonic. Murphy was nursing a beer.

"You found everything?" Murphy asked.

I'd put everything into a manila envelope while I was at my house. "Here you go. I had to make copies of the papers, and he's short one passport."

"What happened?"

I replayed my encounter with Cochran, and Murphy started laughing. "Way to be a super sleuth, Jackson."

"Oh, shut it." I punched him in the arm. "It could have happened to you, too."

"True, enough, except that it never has."

"Piss off." I drank my gin and tonic, pretending to be offended.

"Okay, let's get serious. I can't stay too long. Haithem's onto something. He thinks he knows who the senator is and how he's connected to Abaci Transportation."

"Those pictures showed a shitload of weapons and explosives."

"That's not all. We found evidence of illegal drug shipments."

"Who's the senator and what does he have to do with Alec Covington?"

"We're still connecting the dots. Do you have that picture I gave you a few months ago? The one with Scott and his buddies?"

I nodded.

"One of them is actually Alec Covington. So, it looks like James' group originally had six members."

"Let me guess, he's dead."

"Yes. Looks like he offed himself."

"How?"

"Hanged himself."

"Do you believe that?"

"I don't have enough information to assess it more thoroughly. For now, it was a suicide. Plenty of veterans have done it."

"I took a look at the papers Haithem wanted. They aren't part of this."

"No, he just wanted everything out. Just being cautious."

"What's next?"

"Right now, we've got enough proof to go to my FBI contact in D.C."

"I didn't know you had an FBI contact."

"You still don't know everything about me, love." He polished off his beer and leaned against the back of the stool.

"The pictures you have are for safekeeping." Murphy reached into a black backpack and pulled out a file. "So's this."

I flipped through it. Inside was a listing of the guys who were part of Scott's team, who they worked for, and shipment dates.

"Who's Commander Earley?"

"He was in charge of their unit when they were active. He retired and started Abaci Transportation Corporation. It looks like a big operation, but there's only about one hundred employees on site. When the others retired, one by one, they found their way to Earley. Soon enough, he had them running military-style operations."

"What made them split from Earley?"

"He died."

"How?"

"Executed."

"By who?"

"I'll give you one guess."

"But why would they execute their commander?" I paused and finished my drink while I consider the possibilities. "There's a connection between what happened to Alec Covington and killing Earley, but what?" Murphy was quiet. He knew I was talking it through. "What if Covington found out something he wasn't supposed to?"

"It's a safe bet that they all knew about the smuggling. That's the only reason a guy like Earley would hire an entire ex-special forces type of team."

"I bet some job didn't go down like it was supposed to and now they're getting revenge."

"Definitely possible. You know how to get in touch with James?"

"Yeah."

"Tell him we've got enough to move forward. See if he'll come clean about their part in the deal. There's no way any of them are squeaky clean."

Clive returned, asking if we needed refills.

"No, I'm good," Murphy said. Then to me he added, "I've got to head out." He dropped a few crumpled bills onto the bar. "Keep me informed about James." He stood, kissed my forehead and our eyes met. "Arm's length." I nodded.

After Murphy left, I ordered dinner. It was past eight-thirty, and I was starving. A short time later, Clive placed my usual cheeseburger and fries in front of me. I saw Eddy talking with one of his bouncers near the front door. Whatever it was looked serious.

"Clive?" he walked back over and cleaned the space that Murphy had vacated. "What's up with Eddy?" I tilted my head toward the door.

"I don't know. He's been outa sorts since I got here."

"How'd you end up in here working, anyway?"

"I came in earlier to shoot. Said he was short, and did I want to help out, so I said yeah."

"What's happening with Detrick?"

"He's out on bail. You know Katrina hooked him up."

"Yeah, I know. I spoke with her the other day."

"What'd she say? Are we square?"

"You're covered, and honestly, if Eddy's got you under his wing, there's nothing to worry about. Even Katrina isn't stupid enough to mess with Eddy."

Eddy walked over and took Murphy's spot at the bar. "Clive, grab me a scotch. The good stuff, not the regular shit I serve the youngins."

"What's going on? You seem, I don't know, bothered."

He sighed and said, "It's been one of those days, you know?"

"More than you can imagine."

"You remember my sister-in-law?"

I nodded.

"She's gotten caught up in something and I'm havin to pull her out."

"What is it?"

"Nothing you need to concern yourself with. Not this time."

"How's your niece?"

A while back, Eddy's niece disappeared. She attended the University of Nebraska-Lincoln. It turned out that one her classmates had more than a little crush on her, and tried to kill her because she wasn't interested in him. The guy had a history of similar behavior and a collection of ring fingers in the attic of the house he rented in Lincoln. He was convicted but declared mentally insane. He's serving his sentence at the Nebraska State Pen. They have a special spot for people like him.

"She's doing well. I convinced her to see a counselor, at least for a little while." He sipped his scotch. Holding it in one hand, he swirled it around the ice. "That kid was one fucked-up dude."

"That he was." I handed Clive money for my bill and stood to leave. "Let me know if I can do anything to help. And thanks for looking out for Clive."

"I don't know what you're talking about. I need a little help, that's all." He grinned as the glass met his lips.

CHAPTER EIGHT

I TAPPED ON THE DOOR to Michael Mathews' office and said, "Ehem."

He looked up from his computer screen, and smiling broadly, he said, "This is a pleasant surprise. Come in, please." He gestured to a brown leather couch. "Let me just wrap this up." His attention momentarily returned to his computer. A few seconds later, he joined me on the couch. "What brings you by? I thought you couldn't meet for lunch, today?"

Michael had called a few days ago requesting that we meet, but I'd already planned to have lunch with Cynthia, but something came up and she had to reschedule.

"Michael," I turned to face him, keeping our knees from touching. "I need to ask you a few more questions."

"Ah, I see. So, this isn't a personal visit."

"No."

"Is this about Cal? I was as shocked as everyone else when I heard that he'd been taken in for questioning."

"Have you spoken with him?

"Since the arrest? No, but we don't really talk very often."

"Why were you shocked? Didn't a part of you think that maybe he's guilty?"

"You mean because of Sarah?"

I nodded.

"I believed for a while that it could have been Cal, but I was obviously mistaken." He stood, saying, "Where are my manners? Would you like something to drink? I have a fully stocked bar."

"Water would be great, thanks." I watched him. His gait was tense, not the relaxed, confident one I'd seen the night of the fundraiser, or during our previous date. He returned from the bar with a glass of water for me, and red wine for himself. After handing me my glass, he sat in one of two leather high-back chairs across from me.

"How well do you know Sam Myers?"

"Not well at all, actually. We generally don't move in the same circles except for meeting at the occasional fundraiser."

"But didn't your father have an interest in their firm?"

"Yes, in the beginning, after Sarah and Cal married, my father invested five hundred thousand dollars in the company."

"You had nothing to do with that?"

"No. At the time, I was still working in a middle management position with our company. My father believed I should begin where any other MBA graduate would expect to start. I only moved into an executive position after my parents were killed." He sipped his wine, and continued, saying, "I knew what to expect when I joined my father's company. So, no, I didn't have anything to do with that arrangement and only learned about it after my father's death."

"Did that give your father a controlling interest?"

"Yes, it did, but..." He shifted so that he could set his glass on the table between us. "My father sold his interest to another company when he learned about Cal's escapades."

"What was the name of that company?"

"Erwischt Holdings. Why?"

"Just doing my due diligence, that's all. That must have really upset Cal and Sam."

"Cal, yes. I do remember that."

"What happened?"

"He and Sam came to the office to talk with my father. I was in my father's office when they arrived. As I closed the door to leave, Cal started shouting. I listened for a few minutes."

"What did Sam Myers do?"

"Not much during the time I was listening. Mostly, he made attempts to calm Cal down."

He crossed his legs and leaned back into his chair.

"Dezeray," he didn't like calling me Dez, for some reason. It was endearing, and at the same time, unsettling. The only other people who called me by my full name were my parents. "What are you thinking?"

Switching gears, and completely ignoring his query, I asked, "Michael, Keeney's public defender would really like to speak with Michelle. Have you spoken with her, again?"

He uncrossed his legs and smoothed his pants before reaching for his glass. He lingered a minute, taking in the aroma of the wine before answering. Stalling.

"Yes, I tried to reach her." Lines etched across his forehead.

I might have believed him if his head hadn't moved left to right when he responded. So far, I'd counted at least two blocking gestures, a cleansing of the hands, and now this.

"I've left her several messages. Honestly, Dezeray, when Michelle doesn't want to talk, she simply doesn't answer her phone or return calls." No left to right head movement. What he said was probably an accurate assessment of his sister's behavior.

"When you spoke with her the first time, did you give her my contact information?"

"Yes, of course." The head movement was back. No, he didn't.

"Did you give her Keeney's public defender's contact details?"

Yes, yes, Nope. The only questions I had now were why was Michael lying to me about contacting Michelle, and what was he trying to hide? Or protect? My smile, something honed over years of learning to deceive people, put him at ease. His shoulders relaxed. I checked the time on a clock in his office.

"I don't want to keep you. I'm sure you have work to do." I stood, as did he.

"Yes, thank you. My schedule is a bit tight this afternoon. If I want to survive the meetings, I need to get something to eat."

"Well, I'll let you get to it, then."

He walked me to the door. "I'd love to have dinner with you this weekend." A genuine smile. After all the starts and stops during our meeting, I didn't expect this. Maybe he was simply conflicted. He definitely was protecting someone, and that someone was his sister. But why?

"That would be nice. I'll let you know." I heard the door close behind me. I learned a lot during this meeting and needed to let it marinate. My favorite mind-processing food is pizza. I headed to Zio's on Dodge Street.

The hostess recognized me and knew that I preferred a booth where I could see everyone entering the restaurant. I'd made a mental note to do a background check on her when I first realized she knew this about me. Not because I thought she was a danger. Far from it. She was just a University of Nebraska-Omaha student making ends meet. I was more curious about her potential as an investigator.

"DALTON, I WANT YOU to find everything you can about Erwischt Holdings."

"Anything else, Ms. Jackson?"

"Yeah, has Cochran been around?"

"He did stop by to ask about Haithem's passports. He also mentioned that some were missing from the cache you turned into the Security Department."

Shit. How the hell did he even know? For now, my plan was avoidance. I didn't really need to work at the Lincoln office.

"Dalton, I'm going to be working from my home office for the foreseeable future."

"Got it, Ms. Jackson."

"Let me know as soon as you have more details about Erwischt."

"Of course."

"And Dalton, while you're at it, see what you can find out about Sam Myers. I might have overlooked something where he's concerned."

"Like what?"

"His relationship with his partner for one. It's dysfunctional to say the least. Myers doesn't trust Bridgeton at all. So why go into business with him in the first place?"

"People have done stranger things."

"Maybe, but a business partnership? That seems like a risky thing to do."

"What's Mr. Bridgeton like?"

"Narcissistic sex addict who doesn't think too much about what other people need or want."

"What do you already know about Mr. Myers?"

"Not much beyond schooling. He strikes me as the passive-aggressive type, though."

"Those people are the worst to deal with."

"Yeah, I prefer the direct approach."

I left Dalton to work his magic while I visited Do Space on the corner of Seventy-second and Dodge Streets. It hadn't been open very long and rather than research Myers in my Jeep, I thought being in an actual workspace could prove to be useful and more comfortable.

Do Space is an ultra-modern technological space that provides members meeting space, access to computers of all types, classes, three-dimensional printing, and a laser printer. I didn't know whether I'd ever need to use one of those, but it was nice to know where I could, just in case.

The interior is bright and spacious. I passed a few meeting rooms enclosed by glass walls and continued to the back. Several rows of long, white desks occupied the area with about a hundred desktop computers. A red-orange wall along the length of this part of the space read: Do something great today. I turned the corner and kept walking until I reached a casual seating section with Ikea-style lime-green couches lining a few walls, and white tables with matching chairs. The color scheme was cheery with bold accents of blue, red, yellow, and orange. There were a few too many people for my liking, so I returned to the front where I'd seen a few black butterfly chairs and plopped down, my back to the bank of computers and with an outside view. I settled in and turned on my tablet.

After an hour of skimming articles from the *Midlands Business Journal* and the *Omaha World-Herald* for any information related to Sam Myers, I came across an interesting piece from the *Daily Nebraskan*, the University of Nebraska-Lincoln student paper. It was dated twelve years prior. A female student named Jessica Myers had committed suicide, and her brother, Sam Myers, had provided a quote about her for the paper. The entire article was less than eight hundred words and was intended to provide students access to helplines and other resources if they were depressed. My phone vibrated and I saw that it was Cynthia.

"Hey, Dez. I was able to meet up with Bridgeton. When can we get together? I have a few articles to finish up and an interview, but after that, I'm free."

"How about five thirty at Brazen Head?"

"Sounds good. I'll see you, then."

As soon as the line disconnected, the phone vibrated again. This time it was Dalton.

"Ms. Jackson, Mr. Myers had a sister."

"I know, Dalton, I was just reading about her."

"His sister was dating Cal Bridgeton while they were attending UNL."

"Go on."

"You obviously know what happened to her, but Sam Myers didn't join that fraternity that they both belonged to until after his sister's death. That's where he met Bridgeton. I took a look at his course schedule for the semester directly after Jessica Myers died. He changed it to more closely match Bridgeton's. They had four classes together which..."

"Put him in an even better position to watch Bridgeton. But why?" I asked, more to myself than to Dalton, but he answered anyway.

"You said that Bridgeton is a sex addict. What if that behavior started during college?"

"And Jessica Myers was one of his conquests. Oh, this isn't good. Myers has a grudge and Bridgeton has no clue what's happening."

"What is happening, Ms. Jackson?"

"I haven't put it all together, yet, but I'm guessing that Myers is setting Bridgeton up, somehow. Maybe it's the Briggs murder? I don't know."

"You think Myers killed Briggs and pinned it on Bridgeton?"

"It's possible. He knows everything about Bridgeton's habits. And he knew Briggs. She wouldn't have felt threatened by him. Hell, she was probably having sex with Myers." The minute the words came out of my mouth, I knew it was more than possible. If Myers really had it in for Bridgeton, then what better way to get him?

"Did you find out anything about the holding company?"

"That's even more interesting. So far, I haven't been able to identify all of the owners, but the company was formed shortly after Bridgeton and Myers. Its primary address is in Germany."

"What leads you to believe there's more than one owner?"

"My German is a little rusty, but I read a few documents that appear to reference two people. I've asked the Translation Department to check what I've discovered so far."

"Okay, what's the interesting part?"

"Do you know what Erwischt means?"

"No."

"Gotcha."

AFTER MY ENLIGHTENING conversation with Dalton, my phone rang again. This time it was Charlie. I was feeling very popular.

"Dez, you're gonna seriously owe me for this one. You know how I feel about dogs."

"What are you talking about?"

It was true; Charlie hated dogs, especially small ones. He never told me why, but once, while we were breaking into a dealer's house in Miami, a rat terrier surprised us. I'd never heard someone scream the way Charlie did. He jumped up onto a table to get away from the thing. Charlie's a well-built guy. The table crashed to the floor and the terrier started licking his face. I laughed so hard, I cried. To this day, I give him shit about it.

"Your friend, Michelle, is staying with a guy who has a f'ing dog. And not just any damn dog, it's got one of those smooshed up faces and lots of fur."

"A Pekingese?"

"I don't give a shit what it is. I had to punt the damn thing into a room and close the door."

"Please tell me that you didn't actually punt the dog."

"No, dammit, but I wanted to. I was able to coax it into another room with a treat. I'm like the goddamn UPS delivery guys, now. Always carrying a bag of dog treats. I swear I smell like bacon twenty-four-seven."

"That's smart. I think I'll steal that idea."

"Yeah, whatever. Lucky for you, I found something during my ordeal."

"Go on."

"Michelle, or whoever she is, has a box of journals. Ya know I love it when people keep a record of the shit they do. It makes my job that much easier."

"Journals?"

"Yeah, there's seven."

"And did you happen to read them?"

"You bet your ass I read them. Skimmed, really."

"Dramatic pauses aren't helpful, Charlie."

"Most of it was generally not useful to your current situation, but she does spend a fair amount of time referencing "him." I'm taking that to be a boyfriend or a husband."

"What does she say?"

"From the beginning of the journals she thinks he's cheating. She doesn't specifically say this him is cheating on her until in a later journal. Then, by the seventh book, she's writing about leaving Omaha. I think there's a journal missing, though. The dates aren't lining up."

"Do any of the entries mention Sam Myers?"

"None that I read."

If they were Michelle's diaries, I would've expected at least a mention of Myers, since they dated. Why would Michelle take all of Sarah's diaries before leaving Omaha?

"What else does she say about him?"

"She loved him, but at some point, I got the impression that she didn't."

"What gave you that impression?"

"By the last journal, her writing isn't as angry. Before that, there's a lot of cursing and "I'm going to tell him that I know" language. But, by the seventh, the focus is leaving Omaha, traveling to France, and a few other places. She doesn't bring him up again until an entry about Buenos Aires."

"Does she mention her brother, Michael?"

"She told him something when they met, but she isn't specific in the journal. She wrote, "I told Michael. And I know he'll keep my secret." It's like she was worried someone might read her journals later."

"Can't imagine why she'd worry about that."

He laughed. We read everything when we break into someone's place. If there are bills laying around, we read them. Diaries? Absolutely.

"Hey, Charlie? When you snatched the journals, did you bag 'em?"

"Of course. Why?"

"See if you can lift prints."

"All right. What are you thinking?"

"It's just something Haithem's assistant reminded me about."

"Oh, yeah? What's that?"

"Identical twins aren't actually identical."

BACK IN MY JEEP, I grabbed a snack package of trail mix from my cooler before driving to Brazen Head. I was only five minutes from there, but I didn't want to order any food until Cynthia showed up. We could split the Irish Nachos. She loved them. My favorite appetizer was the Gaelic Hot Wings, but she didn't like the mess factor.

I pulled into the already-crowded parking lot. Brazen Head is in a strip mall, so the availability of parking can sometimes be an issue if you're trying to park closer to your destination. I didn't like parking at one end or the other and then hoofin it to the pub, but today looked as if it was going to be one of those days.

Happy hour was in full swing. People enjoying late lunch meetings or skipping out of work early occupied several of the tables and surrounded the bar. I gave a nod to Mick, one of the regular bartenders. He was from Dublin. I edged passed a few people smackin back shots.

"What can I get you, Dez?"

"A chardonnay. Thanks, Mick."

He left, returning a few seconds later with my wine. "You make your way to Dublin, yet?"

"Not yet. Maybe next year."

"Let me know and I'll hook you up with my family. They've got a B&B. Give you discount." He hurried away to help a customer at the other end of the bar.

I took a corner table in the back and waited for Cynthia. I was early and didn't expect her for another thirty minutes.

"Dez?"

I knew the voice without looking in his direction. Scott James sat across from me, a Guinness in one hand and a plate of hot wings in the other.

"Want some?"

"No, thanks." Yes, but not his. "What are you doing here?"

"Craving." He pointed at the plate. "You?"

"Meeting someone."

"Oh."

"She'll be here in a bit, but since you're here, how about you tell me about Commander Earley?"

Scott's eyes narrowed.

"What about him?"

"Murphy and Haithem know you and the others worked for him after you all left the military. We also know what Abaci Transportation Corporation is doing."

"You've done well. What do you need from me?"

"Alec Covington."

"What about him?"

"What happened? Him killing himself doesn't seem to fit and Commander Earley dying a short time after that can't be a coincidence."

"It's not."

"Tell me what happened."

He finished his scotch. Setting the glass onto the table, his middle finger circled the rim. He was debating how much to tell me. I recognized the look from months of dating each other. Whenever he wasn't sure what to say, he'd get a small wrinkle between his brows.

"We didn't know about the arms or the explosives. Not initially. Alec found out."

"And that's why he was killed."

Scott nodded. "Commander Earley ordered the hit."

"How did you find out what Alec knew?"

"One of the guys found information in a lockbox in Alec's apartment. There were copies of files and a senator's name. None of it made sense until..."

"Until you interrogated Earley."

"Before that, we broke into his office and found the original files that Alec had discovered, but there was a lot more, including the information that we gave you about Savannah."

"But why kill the Commander? You had evidence."

"That was for Alec and these people." He reached into his jacket pocket and pulled out a picture. He placed it onto the table in front of me and pointed at the man in the photo. "That man deserved what he got. He was an arm's dealer. But the family wasn't part of the deal."

"Earley ordered you to kill them?"

He nodded.

"We executed them, set the entire place on fire, and left. After that, Alec found the files, and then the Commander had him killed."

"How is this connected to Savannah?"

"It's the senator."

"Who is he?"

"Carmichael Richie."

"From Virginia?"

"Yes. He keeps dirt on a lot of people."

"But why Savannah?"

"Not Savannah, Dez. Your father."

"This is insane. What does my father have to do with Senator Richie?"

"That's what we wondered, too. We spent a lot of time checking into all the possible connections, and finally found one. Your father was responsible for Richie's son going to the Brig at Camp Pendleton."

"For what?"

"Rape and assault of a minor. But that's not why Richie went after your father. At least, that's not the primary reason."

"What was?"

"Richie's son died in prison. He was killed by another inmate."

"Richie blames my father and had my sister killed."

"That's what we believe happened. The evidence we collected doesn't tie the senator to the Abaci deals. All it does is show that he keeps information on people. What we need is proof that he partnered with Commander Earley. If Murphy and Haithem can do that, then we can move forward and expose the senator."

"Do you know who he hired to kill my sister?"

"No, we don't. That detail wasn't in the file, but there was something else."

"What?"

"We think he might have killed your mother, too."

I let that sink in for a minute. My mom died in a hit-and-run. There wasn't anything suspicious about it. That sort of shit just happens, but it never sat well with me.

"What makes you think that?"

"The senator can't go after your father directly, but he can target each of you. And from what I've learned about him, he enjoys dragging the drama out. He gets off on it. Most of our missions involved letting the person know why we were targeting them. We'd leave them with a gift from him; something only they'd understand. But in your sister's case, he didn't do that. It was as if he was saying he wasn't finished."

"But no one has ever gone after either of my brothers."

"That you know of."

I thought back. There were a few close calls with both of them over the years, but nothing I would have flagged as intentional.

"You think he's targeting my entire family to make my father suffer?"

"That's exactly the kind of man he is. And your new friend, the one I saw the other night, probably works for him. But he's gotten more careful over the years. Your sister's murder was shortly after the death of his son. His emotions were raw and he lashed out. The person he hired was a pro, but he wasn't without his flaws."

Scott reached into his jacket pocket again and handed me a piece of paper. "This is what killed your sister."

"This is the drug?"

"You, or more likely Haithem, can track the sales of that drug during the time Savannah was murdered. You do that, and you might get lucky enough to find your killer."

I saw Cynthia near the bar and waved. She walked over, glass of wine in hand.

"Scott," she greeted him curtly. Cynthia didn't know all the circumstances surrounding the death of my romantic involvement with him. She didn't need to. All that mattered was that she and I were friends and he pissed me off.

Scott grabbed the picture, returned it to the safety of his pocket and stood to leave.

"You can have the rest of the wings."

CYNTHIA KNEW BETTER than to push me about Scott, so she left it alone and took the seat he'd occupied. She slid the plate of wings closer to me. A server stopped to take our appetizer order and I requested another glass of wine. This time, a Merlot. I noticed Mick looking our way.

"You have an admirer." My head tilted to the right. Cynthia smiled and flipped her long, dark hair over her left shoulder so that she could take a quick look.

"Ah, Mick, my fine Irish friend."

"Why don't you ask him out?"

"You know me better than that." In the year or so since we'd met, I'd never known her to ask a man out. Not even for lunch. That's supposed to be the safe date. We differed in our approach to men, but in most other things, we agreed.

"He's obviously interested in you."

"Then he should make his move," she said, and sipped her wine.

"Maybe I'll give him a little nudge."

Setting her glass back down, she said, "You could do that."

Our Irish nachos arrived, and we dug in, both apparently famished.

"I love these a little too much," Cynthia said, wiping her mouth with her napkin.

I'd started in on the wings.

"Bridgeton is a handsome man. I hadn't seen him in person for a long time, and even then, it was from a distance – probably at a fundraiser or something. You were right about him."

"How's that?"

"All I did was put myself in front of him at the gym and let nature take its course. Before I was off the treadmill, he'd come over, asking if I'd like to get a smoothie." Another sip of wine to wash down another chip covered in cheesy, meaty goodness. "That was the easy part."

"What happened?"

"It didn't take him long to remember that he'd seen me before, or at least my picture next to my byline for all of the articles I wrote about his former wife. I was surprised that he didn't bolt right away."

"He probably had some curiosity about how you'd cover the current situation."

"He said as much, actually, but I assured him that it's being covered by another reporter."

"Really?"

"No, but he doesn't know any better."

Lying was an area Cynthia and I shared in common. If it served the greater good, we were fine with it. If it happened to also serve us in some way, that was okay, too. It was all part of the job.

"I told him I was covering the Keeney case and would appreciate his perspective now that eyes would no longer be on him about his wife."

"I can't believe he bought that line of bullshit."

She shrugged. "I'm that good." She pushed her appetizer plate away and leaned her elbows onto the table. "I think I might explode. I'll be right back." She headed in the direction of the bathroom. While she was gone, I stepped up to the bar and got Mick's attention.

"Hey Mr. Smooth, you could ask her out." His cheeks flushed and he looked down sheepishly.

"That obvious?"

I shook my head. "She's not going to approach you. That's not her style."

"What do you think I should do?"

"Send her flowers or something. Not roses. That's too much. Something simple and tickets to see a movie or maybe a play. Then, call her to make sure she received the gift."

"Really? Don't you think that's, I don't know, a bit much?"

"Not if you want to get to know her better." I strolled back to my table and waited for Cynthia to return.

After a few minutes, she came back to the table, but seemed off.

"What's wrong?" I asked.

"Oh, I was just checking messages. It sounds like the police might have another suspect in the Briggs' case."

"Who?"

"My source didn't say. I'm going to check back, later."

"All right, so back to Bridgeton. What did you find out?"

"He was uncharacteristically forthcoming about his relationship with Michelle. I guess he doesn't care now that Keeney's been charged. He said the affair began about a year into his marriage to Sarah and that it was an on-again, off-again arrangement."

"When Michelle started seeing Myers, what did he think?"

"That seemed to amuse him. After she ended it with Myers, he started sleeping with her, again." She paused to take a drink. "I have to say that the entire conversation was creepy strange. He's definitely narcissistic. The entire time we spoke, it was as if he was bragging about his ability to have his way with women. He carried on about the success of his firm, and that Sarah's death hadn't damaged his finances in any significant way. It made my skin crawl."

"What about when Michelle left Omaha? Did he say anything about that?"

"According to him, he didn't care. By then he was back to seeing Briggs more regularly."

"So, he talked about Briggs?"

"No, not in any detail."

"Do you think he's capable of murder?"

"I don't have any proof, but yeah, I think he is. I've covered a lot of murder cases, Interviewed witnesses, family, suspects. Sometimes, I just get a bead on someone, you know what I mean?"

I nodded. "More often than I'd like to, actually."

"Well, it doesn't matter what you or I think Bridgeton is capable of doing. It appears that the police have a different idea."

"Unless, or until we find something else, but I haven't ruled out Michelle or Myers. Michelle had motive. Her sister knew about the affair and threatened to confront Bridgeton, which also happens to give him motive."

"What motive did Myers have?"

"I'm still piecing it together, but I think it might have something to do with his sister. Bridgeton dated her during college."

"Three suspects and none of them are James Keeney."

"Nope."

We both sat silently for a few minutes thinking about what we knew and didn't know.

"I've got a friend checking something out for me in New Orleans. Depending on what he finds, this case could get blown wide open. And you'll be right there to cover it."

We raised our glasses and said, "Cheers."

THE NEXT DAY, I STOPPED at Bridgeton and Myers to ask Daniel a few questions about Sarah and Michelle. Since he knew both of them, or at least had seen both of them a few times, I was curious what he noticed. If there was one thing I'd learned about Daniel it was his keen sense for what was going on around him. His level of situational awareness at work was off the charts good.

I exited the elevator and saw him on the phone behind his desk. He raised a finger, indicating that he'd be a minute. Call finished, he sighed dramatically, and said, "Reporters. They just keep calling."

"Do you have a few minutes to spare?"

He checked his watch. "I can do better than that. It's snack time. Let's go to the break room." I followed him down a hallway and past several offices, to the end where Myers' office was located. The break room was just before it.

"Is he in?"

Daniel's eyes widened and his head bobbed up and down. "And he's in a strange mood."

We walked into the break room and out of earshot of other employees. Daniel opened the refrigerator and removed a small container of yogurt.

"Do you want anything?"

"No, I'm good. Thanks. Daniel, what kind of mood?"

He joined me at a table in the corner.

"He's agitated. He heard the news about Ms. Briggs. Did you hear about that?"

"Apparently, I'm missing a few details."

"Well, the police said they're investigating new leads in the case. Mr. Bridgeton isn't a suspect. At least not for the moment. When Mr. Myers heard it on the news, I happened to be in his office at the time, his face became red. Like a radish, I swear! When I asked if he was okay, he was calm as could be, like nothing happened." He opened the container. "It was really strange. I've never seen Mr. Myers upset before." He took a bite and his eyes closed as he savored his snack. Then his eyes popped open. "That's not why you wanted to talk with me. So sorry to dump that on you."

"That's okay." I loved it when people mind dumped. "I'm just wondering if you could tell me more about Sarah and Michelle."

"Like what?"

"I realize that you might have seen Sarah more often than Michelle, but did you ever notice anything different about them?"

He'd finished the yogurt and set the container, with the plastic spoon inside, on the table in front of him. "They were identical as far as looks go, but Sarah was more reserved than Michelle. Michelle liked attention. I remember one year at our annual holiday party, Michelle was invited. She took up a lot of space on the dance floor. Mrs. Bridgeton never did that."

"I've discovered that Mr. Bridgeton was having an affair with Michelle."

Daniel's expression didn't change immediately, but then he said, "I knew it!"

"What did you know exactly?"

"One night I thought Mrs. Bridgeton had come into the office, and I remember thinking how unusual it was for her to do that, but now I know it was Michelle. That makes so much more sense."

"Why do you think it was Michelle?"

"She tried to play it off like she was her sister, but, and I know this might seem an odd thing for a person to notice, but she didn't walk the same way Mrs. Bridgeton did. Michelle had sort of a strut, like a prowling lioness. Definitely not Mrs. Bridgeton's style."

"After the murder, did you see Michelle?"

"Now that you mention it, I did. She came to the office to see Mr. Bridgeton. I think she left Omaha shortly after that."

"Thanks, Daniel." I stood to leave. "You've been a great help."

"Anytime," he said and got up to follow me out. "Ms. Jackson?"

I stopped and turned around to see that Daniel was pointing in the direction of Sam Myers' office. Through the glass, we could see that Sam Myers was on the phone. His face was several shades redder than his usual slightly tanned state, and he was pacing.

"That's what I was telling you. Not normal." We continued down the hall.

CHAPTER NINE

AFTER LEAVING DANIEL, I left a message for Murphy and made my way to Lincoln to visit Keeney. He was in better shape this time and seemed in good spirits.

"Ya know, if they can't pin the murder on me, I can do my dime, and be on my way."

"That's still a hefty chunk."

"Beats life. Mazy wants to move back south. She's tired of the cold."

"Nebraska winters are a bitch, but I prefer having four distinct seasons."

"Me, too, and there's more jobs here."

"Jobs?"

"Yeah, I'm gonna get me a real job. Maybe in security."

I laughed. "You might not be too far from the mark on that idea. Who better to hire than an expert at B&E?"

He smiled, revealing his stained teeth. I noticed one had a small chip that I hadn't seen before.

"Everything going all right in here?"

He shrugged. "It is what it is."

"Keeney, I've got good news."

He sat up straighter in his chair and rested his forearms on the table.

"I've got three viable suspects in the Sarah Bridgeton murder and you're not one of them."

"Shit. I know I ain't one of them. Who ya got?"

"Cal Bridgeton, Michelle Mathews, and Sam Myers."

"I saw that Bridgeton guy on the news. Police think he killed some lady named Briggs, right?"

I nodded. "They're investigating his connection and some other people. If he's good for the Briggs' death, then they might look at him again for his wife's murder. We all know he was there that night, but I think he might have been there earlier than the police discovered during the original investigation."

"And the other two?"

"Michelle wasn't a stable woman. She was jealous of her sister and started having an affair with Bridgeton after Sarah married him. I think I told you that they might have been seeing each other. Now I have confirmation directly from Bridgeton. And the police never knew about their affair. They also didn't know that he's a sex addict."

Keeney's mouth dropped open, and then he said, "What? You're shittin me? Of all the problems to have, I'd take sex addict any day of the week."

"Sam Myers' sister dated Bridgeton during college and committed suicide when he broke it off. Myers certainly has a motive for screwing up Bridgeton's life."

"Who do you think set me up?"

"Let's be clear about one thing; no one set you up. You did break into the Bridgeton house. It was more a matter of being in the wrong place at the wrong time. You weren't careful and your prints showed up, so don't act like you're completely innocent here."

He shifted his gaze away and squirmed in his chair.

"Keeney?" He looked back at me. "You're probably going to get another chance, so I hope you're serious about taking it. You've got money to make a move, and you could get a real job."

"You know people don't like to hire convicts."

I couldn't argue with that. A lot of businesses wouldn't want a guy, known for stealing, working in their business.

"As for who I think actually murdered Sarah Bridgeton? I don't like to speculate. I like proof. And right now, I don't have anything tying any of them directly to the scene. All I've got are theories."

James Keeney breathed deeply, pushed his chair back and stood up. "Guard!" I grabbed my satchel and followed him into the hall. Shoulders hunched and hands in his pockets, Keeney made his way back to his cell.

"Keeney."

He looked back over his shoulder.

"One of my theories is right. I'll find the evidence. Just stay out of trouble until I do."

Part of me felt sorry for James Keeney. He wasn't a bad guy. Not really. He had genuine talent when it came to breaking into houses. His public defender gave me more information about his background that made me understand why he chose this particular career path. None of it was a surprise. He was raised by his mother and didn't know his father. He graduated from school, but barely, and reading wasn't his strength. His PD pegged him at about a third or fourth grade reading and comprehension level, but said he was great with numbers. And apparently, he had a good memory for details.

His work history was sketchy, mostly taking on labor jobs or washing dishes. Honestly, he possessed traits that could be enhanced with the right training. Tracer International wasn't above hiring a convict. It all depended on their skillset, whether the person could be trained, and what crimes they committed. A few B&Es was a good resume-builder as far as Tracer was concerned. One less thing that had to be taught.

I bypassed stopping into the office so that I could avoid running into Steve Cochran. The last thing I wanted to do was get caught up trying to explain Haithem's missing passports. I'd left a message with Haithem's boss asking him to deal with Cochran. He knew Haithem was underground for the time being.

All my communication the past few months was with Murphy, so I didn't really know how Haithem was doing. He was always close to his family, and I suspected that this situation was more difficult for him than he'd let Murphy know. But Murphy had no choice but to take Haithem when he did. He'd been ordered to kill him and when Murphy figured out that the order was connected to Abaci Transportation, and ultimately, some senator, he got tired of following orders. If Haithem hadn't been spending so much time helping me to investigate what Scott and his buddies were feeding me, he wouldn't have become a target.

This was all weighing on my brain as I drove the hour back to Omaha. After a while, I had to stop running through things in my mind. I popped a CD into the player and soon my head was bopping to the reggae beats of Bob Marley.

WHEN I ARRIVED HOME, I saw Murphy's Harley parked in my driveway. He tucked it close to the garage so that I could still pull in. When I opened the door, the enticing aroma of Thai curry beckoned me to the kitchen. I dropped my satchel onto the table and hurried in that direction. I was starving, but I hadn't even realized it until I smelled the food. Murphy was unpacking the take-out while Godfrey lay near the back door gnawing on the remains of a steak bone.

"Beers are in the fridge. I picked up some of that Lucky Bucket IPA you got me hooked on. Thanks for that, by the way." He walked over, kissed my forehead, and grabbed utensils from the drawer next to the fridge.

We sat at the small 50s-era table, filling our plates with rice, and green curry with shrimp. He'd also picked up one of my favorite appetizers: fresh spring rolls.

"You stopped at the Thai and Vietnamese place? They're not anywhere near each other." Salween Thai Restaurant was on NW Radial Highway, north of Dodge Street, and Saigon was off of 120th and Center Streets, south of Dodge Street.

"Anything for you, love." He winked at me and popped open his beer. "Tell me what James had to say. Hopefully something useful."

I filled him in on the previous night's discussion, pausing periodically for bites of my curry.

"It's nice to finally know the senator's name. Haithem had it narrowed down to two."

"What's next?"

"The senator has done a great job trying to hide his connection to Commander Earley and Abaci Transportation, but Haithem found something in an offshore account. The senator has made and received several large payments throughout the years. Some of the payments he received are tied to shipments originating from Abaci Transportation. Haithem was able to track some of the other payments to an account belonging to a man named Victor Hess. He's military-trained, but never joined up."

"It sounds as though you and Scott have the proof you need to nail the senator."

"Looks like it."

"But?"

"Haithem also found trails leading to Scott's group, McIntyre, and to me. The orders we carried out would become public knowledge. And I'm guessing there'd be other consequences."

"Prison."

"Most likely. There's not a lot of love for people in my line of work when secret information becomes known."

"The senator doesn't actually know who you are, though."

"No, but my handler does, and he'd get exposed right along with the senator if we go public."

"The Feds would make a deal for what you and Scott know."

"Probably, but there aren't any guarantees."

I reached for one of the spring rolls, and sank my teeth into the soft rice paper wrapped around glass noodles, shrimp, lettuce and basil. It was the basil that made the experience come together. I washed it all down with a swig of my beer.

"Haithem could make your information disappear," I said.

"Yeah, he and I discussed that option."

"And?"

"And I'm all for it, but if we're going to do it, James and his last remaining partner need to be on board. We can't have any loose ends."

"Why wouldn't he want it erased? I'm sure prison wouldn't be his preferred way to spend the next twenty or so years of his life."

"Guilt can make a man do strange things."

"I'll talk to him."

"Everything would be gone. We'd have new identities. He'd have to disappear to where no one knows him."

"Haithem can engineer anything you guys need for your new identities. Job histories. Everything."

Murphy played with the bottle cap from his beer. "I know. And it's not like I haven't done it a million times before, but James hasn't. It's not an easy life. He's dabbled, but he hasn't had to live it for extended periods of time. And I'm betting his partner, Remington, hasn't either. They're probably thinking that they'll be able to go back to something familiar when this is over. That ain't gonna happen no matter what they decide."

I'd left my cell phone in my satchel and could hear it ringing. "I'll be right back."

It was Scott, but I missed it. A second later, a text came through. I returned to the kitchen.

"What happened? You're about as pale as me."

"It was Scott. I think something happened."

Murphy stood up and took the phone from me.

"What the?" The text said, "Hummel Park."

"Someone's gotten to him. What else could this mean?"

"Let's go."

Murphy grabbed his backpack, and I followed him out the door.

"I'm right behind you."

We raced through the streets of Omaha to the northeast side of town and to Hummel Park. We wound our way through the forest, going up and down narrow roads until we reached a parking area. At the bottom of a long series of steps was an area that always reminded me of a Roman stage made of stone and columns. Scott lay on the slab not moving. I ran to him while Murphy, gun already poised to shoot, canvassed our surroundings. Scott's phone rested on his chest.

"What happened?"

Scott struggled to speak. I removed my leather jacket and placed it beneath his head. Blood poured from his shoulder; there were three holes in the front of his jacket. I unzipped it. A vest. He'd worn his vest.

"Did you see who it was?"

"Remington."

"What?" I applied pressure to his shoulder wound; blood coated my hands. "Murphy!"

He ran over, opened his backpack, and removed a towel. "Use this." Then he took out a medical kit. I watched as he cleaned and bandaged the wound. "Bullet went straight through. It's gonna hurt like hell, but you'll live." He grabbed a large Ziplock plastic bag from his pack, stuffed the bloodied towel and used bandages inside and tossed it onto the center of the pavement. He walked over, lit a match, and let it burn the bag and its contents. After a several minutes, he stomped out the flames and scattered the remains with a swoosh of his right boot.

"Murphy, it was Remington."

Murphy turned back toward me. I was helping Scott sit up. "Your buddy?"

Scott nodded.

"Well, that's a problem."

AS MUCH AS MURPHY DETESTED the idea that Scott James was going to stay at my place, he hated knowing that one of Scott's brothers-in-arms turned on him, even more. That was enough to send him over the edge. I heard the low rumble of his Harley leave my driveway, knowing that in short order Murphy would track Remington down, beat him into submission, and then dispose of him in whatever way he deemed necessary. Scott told us that he and Remington had been staying in a cabin in Hummel Park since early last year.

"Do you usually wear your vest?" I asked as he reclined on the couch. I handed him a beer and set a scotch on the table next to him.

"No, but lately, ever since I found out about the guy tracking you, I figured it would be prudent."

"Always prepared."

"It's the Boy Scout motto." He strained to smile as he shifted his weight to get more comfortable.

"Are you hungry?"

"You're going to cook?" I tossed a pillow at him.

"I'll make ravioli. It's frozen, but the sauce is homemade. Not by me."

"That sounds great. Thanks, Dez."

I left him with the remote to the TV, and his adult beverages, while I went to work in the kitchen. I was still stuffed from the Thai food, so I only made enough for Scott. I grabbed a baguette from the pantry and popped it into the oven. The fact that Remington turned on Scott, and I had a new BFF following me around irritated me. What gave this senator the right to screw with my family just because his son was a good-for-nothing son of a bitch? It didn't. The water had just started to boil. I walked into my office and said out loud, "You want to play? Let's do this." Then, I snatched the bugging device from its spot. I went upstairs to my room and grabbed the second one.

From downstairs, Scott asked, "What are you doing?"

"I'm done with this shit. That senator is truly fucking with the wrong Jackson."

I returned to the kitchen and tossed the bugs into the boiling water.

"Dinner is going to be a little delayed," I shouted from the kitchen.

I GOT UP THE NEXT MORNING feeling pretty damn good about how I handled the bugs. I got cleaned up, let me curls fly loose, dressed in jeans, a red tee that said, "Hit like a girl," and pulled my pointy-toed cowboy boots on. I called them my sexy shit-kickers with attitude. My first stop this morning was going to be Simmons to train. Then, I planned to do some target shooting and knife practice.

Descending the stairs, I saw that Scott was still wiped out on the couch. From the kitchen, Godfrey heard me, and began whining. Before I'd gone to bed, he had found a spot near the end of the couch to keep an eye on Scott.

Breakfast was fried eggs, toast, tea, and a pile of bacon. The loud, rotary ringtone from my phone surprised me; it was six thirty. Dalton knew better than to call at this hour. I read the screen and discovered that it was Charlie.

"Shoot."

"Good morning to you too, sunshine. Rough night?"

"You don't know the half of it."

"I got an interesting result from the prints I lifted from those journals."

"Oh, yeah?"

"I was able to find out that Sarah and Michelle both had their prints floating around the system. Sarah's were printed when she volunteered at a local youth clinic. They ran a background check, including prints. Michelle's were in the system because she got into trouble for shoplifting when she was sixteen. The prints on the journals match Sarah's."

"Okay, so Michelle took all of the diaries."

"No, I don't think so. Even the most current entries in the most recent diary match Sarah's prints."

"Are you saying what I think you are?"

"I'm saying that your girl here in New Orleans is Sarah Bridgeton."

I almost dropped my cell phone.

"Then Michelle is the one who was killed that night. But why?"

"I can't tell you all that. What I can say, without a doubt, is that whoever died that night wasn't Sarah Bridgeton."

Charlie ended the call. I stood in my kitchen, dumbfounded. Then it hit me. Michael Mathews knew Michelle was the one who died that night. I didn't know when he knew, but every ounce of me knew that he did, and he was covering it up. It was too early to call him, so I grabbed my weapons bag from the basement, wrote a note for Scott, and left.

The drive to Simmons was uneventful but took longer than the usual fifteen minutes because of traffic heading downtown. As I wound through the streets of one of the neighborhoods surrounding the business district, the beautiful old brick houses reminded me why I loved this area of town. I would have considered buying a house in this neighborhood if my Great Aunt Violet hadn't left me hers when she died.

I parked along Maple Street and went inside the dojang. A few regulars, or as I preferred to call them, dedicated practitioners, were rolling. I wasn't here for that, though. This morning, I wanted to hit, and hit hard, so I skipped the front of the gym and found my way to the back. Master Simmons came out of his office when he saw me.

"What are we doing this morning?"

"Whatever it takes."

***

BY THE TIME I'D SHOWERED and changed at Simmons, I knew I had a better chance of reaching Michael, so I gave him a call. He had a few meetings this morning but could meet me for lunch. I suggested Pizzeria Davlos off 142nd and Fort Streets. It was a little off the beaten path, and that's what I wanted. He enjoyed being seen. I didn't. Michael wasn't familiar with Davlos, so I texted him the directions.

At eleven forty-five, I was seated at a booth in Davlos, across from a bank of windows. I liked being able to see what or who was coming. From my spot, I had full view of a good portion of the parking lot and the front doors. Normally, I wouldn't be comfortable not being able to see all entry and exit points, but today, my situational awareness was at Spidey Sense level.

Michael entered the pizzeria wearing a tailored navy-blue suit with a coordinated polka-dot tie. I hate polka dots. It was like someone vomited confetti. I smiled and waved when I saw him scanning the restaurant, which by now had filled up. He removed his jacket, folded it in half, and lay it on the bench before sliding in across from me.

"Interesting choice," he said with a tentative smile.

"They have a good wine list. I'm sure you'll be able to find something you like."

A server stopped at our table to deliver water for Michael.

"We're ready to order," I said. Michael stared at me in silent bewilderment. I ordered a thin crust, ten-inch meat eater. To him, I said, "You're going to love this. Trust me." I smiled, putting him at ease. "You should order the wine, though. That is your specialty." He did, and the server rushed away to deliver the order to the bartender.

"I'm happy you called," he said. "I've been wanting to get together." I knew he had, and to be honest, if he wasn't part of this case, and lying to me, I might be interested in pursuing something.

"Michael, this isn't a personal lunch."

He sat up straighter and rested his hands in his lap. What the hell was he hiding? Oh, yeah, that little detail about Sarah not being dead.

"What's this about?"

"Sarah. I know she's the woman in New Orleans." I let that float in the air like a cloud about to turn gray and rain down hail.

"I don't know what you mean." His hands stroked his pants. Then he moved his water glass between us.

"Michael, you don't need to hide anything from me. I know."

"I don't know what you believe that you know, but I can assure you that..."

I raised one of my hands to stop him from continuing. "I have prints matching the woman in New Orleans to a set of diaries. They belong to Sarah, not Michelle, so how about you save me the drama and tell me when you knew?"

He sighed and leaned his back against the booth. "Sarah called me after Michelle's body was discovered. She'd been out walking that night. When she came home, there were police surrounding her house."

"Why didn't she go in?"

"I don't know. She said that she saw what was happening and just left. A day later, she called me. I was devastated, as I'm sure you can imagine, considering your experiences."

That one sentence sent a shock through my body, starting at the base of my spine. "You don't know anything about me."

"Oh, come on. I know your sister was murdered. Swan told me that."

Martial arts teach restraint, which is a good thing when all you want to do is reach across a table and grab a person's throat, but maybe I was still reeling from the night before. I swallowed my anger and pushed on.

"What happened next?"

"Everyone believed that Sarah was dead. And honestly, no one was going to miss Michelle."

"Sarah assumed Michelle's identity and let whoever killed her walk away. Now, James Keeney is set to spend the rest of his life in prison."

"I realize that."

"I don't think you fully appreciate it. You're protecting her, even now. Even when you know that her being alive could reopen this investigation and save Keeney."

"Keeney? You're worried about some lowlife. I'm concerned for my sister's safety. What if it was Cal who killed Michelle, believing that it was Sarah? What then?"

He was right. I still didn't know who killed Michelle, but I did know that it wasn't Sarah. Or at least, I thought so.

"How do you know it wasn't Sarah who killed Michelle?"

"Sarah was angry when she discovered that Michelle had been sleeping with Cal, but then she saw it as a way out."

"A way out? What the hell are you talking about?"

"Sarah knew about all of the other women. She was embarrassed, to say the least. She didn't want to be known as that woman whose husband slept with anything with a pulse and breasts."

"If anything, that gives her motive."

"It would, except that she stopped at a convenience store that night to buy a bottle of water. The store had footage of her entering and leaving. It's time stamped."

"You said 'had.'"

"I have it. When she told me what happened, I had Dick Swan take care of it."

"Do you have any idea how screwed up all of this is?"

He nodded.

"I need her to meet with Keeney's PD. She's got to tell her what happened that night."

"She won't."

"You need to convince her."

"What if I can't?"

"Then I'll drag her sorry ass back here myself."

"HAVE YOU FOUND REMINGTON?" I asked.

Murphy called to check in and to make sure nothing negative was happening at my place. That included Scott moving into what he considered to be his territory. I thought the man knew me better than that. I'm not anyone's personal playground.

I'd returned from lunch with Michael angrier than I was when I went to the gym. My plan was to check on Scott, and then go to a range. I hadn't gotten any target practice in yet and squeezing off a few rounds would help me focus. That, and imagining the senator's face as my target.

"No, but I will. He's got to still be in Omaha, or possibly Council Bluffs. I've got a few people helping me out."

I didn't ask who. He wouldn't have told me.

"Scott's moving around better. I redressed the wound, but he needs something stronger than ibuprofen."

"Tell him to suck it up." Murphy hung up.

"That was Murphy?" Scott asked from the couch.

"No word on Remington, yet. Murphy's got more eyes and ears out. I doubt it'll take him long." I grabbed my guns and ammo bag and slinging it over my shoulder, I said, "There's plenty of food in the fridge. Help yourself."

"Where are you going?"

"Target practice." I headed toward the door.

"Dez, you can't go after the guy. You don't even know what he looks like."

"I know that, but when he decides to come out and play, I'm going to be on point. The fact is, I don't want to kill him. He's working for Richie. I know it. There's no other reasonable explanation. And I want information from him." I'd already grabbed the file with the pictures Scott gave me of the guy. I was betting The Lab could enhance the images and give me a little more to go on.

The drive to the range took thirty minutes through traffic and fortunately, the range wasn't busy when I arrived. Tony Shapiro, the owner, checked me in, but didn't strike up a conversation the way he usually did. I was putting out a "don't F with me vibe" that could be felt for miles. I set up and stayed for about an hour before finally feeling the edges smooth out. I packed up, climbed into my Jeep, and checked messages. There was only one and it was from Dalton.

"What did you find, Dalton?"

"Erwischt Holding belongs to Sam Myers, and right now he's positioned to take complete control of Bridgeton & Myers. I did more checking into Bridgeton & Myers' finances. They're seriously leveraged, and Bridgeton's personal portfolio is tanking."

"Let me guess, Myers is sitting pretty well?"

"Oh, yeah. The man's worth millions."

"So, Sam Myers is out for revenge."

"Looks like it."

"All right, let's cross him off the list for the time being. If all he's out to do is take Bridgeton down a few notches, who am I to stop him."

I love it when Karma comes knockin and assholes get their due. Without Myers to worry about, I could focus on Sarah and Bridgeton. One of them killed Michelle. Despite Michael's insistence that it couldn't be Sarah, I wasn't so sure. In my experience, a woman scorned is pretty tough to beat, as far as motives go. Maybe she was trying to set him up and get her sister at the same time. I'm not ready to let her walk without answering a few questions, that's for damn sure. The only question was, 'how?' Getting her to Omaha wasn't going to be easy.

Calling Dick Swan would be a mistake because he still worked for Michael, so I called Charlie for a quick brainstorming session.

"Why don't you see if the public defender can subpoena her? You've got the diaries and fingerprints. I would think that it's at least enough to warrant a look from the PD's office, even if their budget is tight. They've got to follow the leads."

"It might not be enough."

"Yeah, but that's not your call. Give the PD the info and let her decide what direction to go. In the meantime, keep pushing the brother. You said he's got a tape showing Sarah at a store. That's evidence that supposedly rules her out as a suspect, but what if it doesn't?"

"If I push him, then he's going to become more resistant. He doesn't want to see his sister go to prison."

"This is his way to ensure that it doesn't happen. You need the tape so that you can help him prove that she couldn't have killed Michelle. Play up the Bridgeton angle."

"Make Michael believe that I think it was Bridgeton?"

"Right now, it could be either one, so convince him that in order to get Bridgeton for the murder of Michelle, you need the tape."

After we finished our back and forth, I knew it was what I needed to do, but my last chat with Michael didn't exactly end well. Dick Swan supposedly had the tape. I could break into his place and find it. But then there's the whole stolen-evidence thing. On the other hand, I could take a look at it, so that I know when she was actually at the store. Maybe Dick Swan would be willing to let me see it. I gave him a call.

"Let me get this straight. Michelle is the dead one?"

"I think so."

"And you're trying to prove that Sarah is still alive?"

"And where she was at the time of the murder."

"She wasn't at her house. I can tell you that. I've reviewed the security tape."

"I just need to see it for myself, so that I know I can rule her out. You know how it is."

"All right."

"I'll be there in thirty minutes."

Dick Swan had everything set up and ready for me to view when I arrived. We played and replayed the tape.

"The murder was believed to have happened between eight-thirty and nine o'clock in the evening. This clearly shows her walking into the store at eight thirty-five and leaving fifteen minutes later," Swan said.

"Why in the world would it take anyone fifteen minutes to buy water?"

"Maybe she was looking at snacks. I don't know, but she wasn't at the house. Their place in Regency is at least a twenty-minute walk from the store. She couldn't have gotten back home and killed Michelle in that time frame."

"She could have jogged it. Or maybe she wasn't really out walking. The only person who said she was out walking that night was Michael."

Dick Swan leaned back in his chair, stroking his beard.

"The only other person who knows what she was doing that night is her."

"You're right. She needs to help clear this up. I'd hate seeing a poor bastard like Keeney going down for something he didn't do. It looks like you've got at least one viable alternative to explain what happened that night," Swan said.

"Two."

"The husband?"

"Yeah. He might have killed Michelle, believing that she was Sarah. If Sarah confronted him about the affairs that could have been enough to set him off. What if he was with Briggs that night as a way to have a backup alibi? He could cop to the affair, and she'd lie to help him cover any time gaps."

"It's possible. I've seen people commit murder for simpler things than this."

"Talk to Michael. We both know that I could give this, and everything else I know to Keeney's PD, and that Sarah would get subpoenaed. If she's not involved, then that could prove to be a bad choice, because that would mean that Bridgeton could get a second chance at her. If she agrees to return, we could keep her hidden for the time being and find out what she knows about that night."

"If she killed Michelle, the only way you're going to get her here is with a subpoena."

"Tell Michael that I believe it was Bridgeton, but that I can't prove it without Sarah's help. I can't imagine that he wouldn't push Sarah to help resolve this, as long as we promised to keep her safe."

Swan agreed to get in touch with Michael, and I was hoping that I'd hear back from either him, or Michael, by the end of the day.

CHAPTER TEN

I ARRIVED HOME FROM Swan's office after seven o'clock. When I opened the door, I expected to see Scott laid out on the couch either sleeping or watching TV. He wasn't. The sweet smell of roasted garlic brought a smile to my face. I breathed it in. Scott had his faults - liar being one of them, but he could do amazing things with food.

"You must be feeling better," I said, walking into the kitchen.

"Some. Cooking keeps my mind from focusing on the pain. How about you?" He had been putting together a salad but turned to look at me.

"Better." I poured a glass of wine from a bottle he'd left open on the counter to breathe. "What are we having?" I sat at the table, glass in hand.

"Poached salmon and linguine with a roasted garlic cream sauce, and mixed green salad tossed in a lemon vinaigrette."

My stomach started doing its happy dance. I missed Scott's cooking.

"You know, I never had a chance to tell you how sorry I am for everything." He'd returned his attention to the food.

"Let's not do this now, okay?"

"I want to make sure I don't leave things unsaid."

The happy dance stopped. He was really going to do this now. I set my glass on the table.

"There's not a lot to say, Scott."

"Yes, there is." He turned back to me. "I love you, Dez. I didn't think that would happen. I didn't expect it to. You were supposed to be my assignment."

"Yes, I remember that part." My neck muscles began to tighten. I reached for my wineglass.

"Being with you during those months proved to me that I wanted more. I didn't want to keep living the life I was. But I had to finish what the team started. I couldn't be honest with you and do that. Believe it or not, I was trying to protect you."

"Protect me? Really? You were using me to get the information you thought you needed so you could get to Richie. How is that protecting me?" My volume increased with each word. Before I realized it, I was on my feet.

"You needed to know about Savannah. And yes, we knew that if you started digging into things, then with your connections to Tracer International..."

"You mean Haithem."

He nodded. "We couldn't approach him directly, but you could, and he will do anything for you." He turned down the heat for the salmon. "You have that effect on the men in your life."

I felt heat rise in my cheeks. I'd never had anyone tell me that before, and I hadn't ever given much thought to how Haithem felt about me. We were pals and training partners, nothing more.

"I never meant to hurt you. I just want to know that you understand that."

"I do understand, but I'm still angry with you, and I can't help that right now." I'd calmed down, but still felt the tightening in my neck, and began rolling my head side to side to loosen up.

"Let me," he said, setting the spatula he'd been using onto the counter.

"No, that's all right." I backed away from him. "I told you before, you don't have those privileges anymore."

He put up his hands and went back to the stove. "Maybe I will again someday."

I took my wineglass and left the kitchen. I couldn't kick him out, but I didn't have to stay in the same room with him. When the food was ready, he found me in the living room.

"At least eat. You can still be pissed at me, but don't let one of your favorite meals go to waste."

Damn, he was playing that card.

"Fine, but we're not revisiting any discussion about us."

"Deal. For now."

I followed him into the kitchen. He'd set the table with a tablecloth that I didn't know I had, and matching napkins. I watched as he plated the food. If he wanted a second career, a restauranteur could be it. Or maybe personal chef. Remembering all the great meals we'd shared at this table; I smiled despite myself.

"What?" he asked as he sat next to me.

"Nothing." I took my first bite of the salmon and linguine. My eyes closed as I inhaled the intoxicating aroma of the garlic sauce.

"Some things never change," I heard Scott remark. I opened my eyes. "Watching you eat is a sensual experience that I never tire of."

"Stop it."

"What? I'm being honest."

"You're flirting with me. This," I pointed back and forth between us, "Ain't gonna happen, so stop it."

"I'm willing to wait for you to forgive me."

"That might be a while."

"I know."

The timer on the oven sounded and Scott stood to check something in the refrigerator. "Ah, perfect," he said, and pulled out a chocolate tart. He set it on the table before grabbing a bowl of strawberries encased in cream, and another bottle of wine from the fridge.

"La piece de resistance." He smiled broadly, as my eyes widened, taking it all in. "It's been too long since we had this."

"You're trying to kill me."

"I'm trying to say that I'm truly sorry. And you mean more to me than I'll ever be able to tell you." He touched my hand. This time I didn't take it away.

"If I have to spend the rest of my life convincing you, then I will."

It was his eyes that finally did me in. Of course, I wouldn't admit it to him. He was going to have to spend a little more time in purgatory.

"Let's just start with dinner."

"That's all I want. A new start."

I pressed play on the remote to my kitchen stereo system and we listened to smooth jazz while we enjoyed his decadent creation. Truth was, I couldn't hate him. He did get me closer to learning what happened to my sister. And he did keep that crazy man from blowing up my Jeep with me inside. But Murphy was back in my life, and I didn't know where that relationship was headed, but we were happy, again.

We cleaned up the kitchen together and decided to take Godfrey for a walk, because we needed the exercise after eating about half the tart. I grabbed my gun, just in case, and holstered it behind my jacket.

"You really think you'll need that?"

"You never know. Do you want yours?"

He smiled, pulled back his jacket and revealed the gun on his hip. We laughed at that. Godfrey danced excitedly as I snapped the leash to his collar. Once we were outside, he pulled me down the stairs to the gate. Scott moved more slowly but caught up. The gate led to an alley that ran along the west side of my property. We walked in silence for a few strides. A cool breeze caused a shiver to crawl up my back and I stopped to zip my jacket. We continued down the alley, noticing that the sky was clear enough to just make out a few stars. It would have been a peaceful, relaxing walk if it weren't for the sound of footsteps in the distance, but not too far behind.

"It's probably nothing," Scott said. "Let's keep walking, turn at the corner, and see what happens."

I nodded.

When we reached the corner, we turned left and waited. The footsteps had sped up. Scott motioned for me to take Godfrey and go into a neighbor's yard while he stepped behind their garage. We waited and listened. The footsteps slowed as they approached the end of the alley. Then whoever it was turned right and continued walking for about half a block before turning back and heading in our direction. His face was obscured by a hood. Something about his walk was familiar.

I stepped out from the neighbor's yard and in front of Murphy.

"What the hell are you doing?"

"I was looking for you. Where's James?"

Scott reappeared from his hiding spot.

"What are you two doing?"

"Taking a walk. What the hell does it look like?" I said.

"Looks like things are about the same with you two. I'm going back to Dez's. I'll meet you there." Scott left us there staring at each other.

"A walk? Really?" Murphy asked as we returned to the alley.

"He made dinner and we needed to walk it off."

"Dinner? He made you dinner? Just like old times, eh?"

"Jealous?"

"Do I need to be?"

When I didn't answer right away, Murphy stopped walking. "What's going on, Dez?"

"Nothing. Really."

"Are you sure?"

"Yes," I said, and started walking again.

"He's smooth. Remember?" He caught up with me. "Don't fall for his line of BS. That's all it is. You're smarter than that."

"I know, Murphy. Stop worrying."

He reached for my hand, pulling me closer to him. His blue-green eyes locked on mine. "You're the only person that matters to me here." His left hand stroked the side of my face, and in that moment, I forgot Scott James.

WHEN WE GOT BACK TO my house, Scott was sitting on the deck, feet propped on the rail, drinking a beer. Godfrey lay near his feet.

"Here," Murphy handed Scott a small piece of paper folded in half. "Your boy Remington is headed toward Sioux City, IA. Any idea why he'd head that direction?"

"He's got family in Minnesota."

"If you want to handle this, call that number. My guy is still on him. You can meet up and tell him what you need."

I was leaning against the rail, arms folded across my chest, taking in the conversation like this was an everyday thing. Truth was, hearing them discuss it, without really discussing it, was disturbing.

"You can't kill him," I said.

They stopped talking and stared at me.

"That's premeditated murder."

"He has to be dealt with," Murphy said. "He knows everything James and his crew did and all about Commander Earley. Senator Richie probably paid him a good amount of change to take out James."

"I know. I get that, but there's got to be another way to deal with him."

Scott's legs hit the deck with a soft *thud*.

Turning his attention toward Scott, Murphy asked, "What are you thinking?"

"He's not going to come at me again, because he knows I'll be watching for him. And I'm betting that the senator has other plans for him. He's not the kind of man who follows through on this kind of payout. He cleans house. Remington is on the run from me and the senator now. I say we capture and detain until we finish setting up the dominoes for the senator."

Murphy was nodding his head as he listened.

"That sounds reasonable," I said. "And better than prison."

"All right, Haithem is getting our aliases established. You hit the road and meet up with Tango."

"I'll drive you back to your cabin," I said.

Murphy's eyebrows raised.

"What? He's going to ride on the back of your Harley?"

MY OFFICE PHONE RANG at nine thirty in the morning. I was hoping it was Michael or Swan. It wasn't.

"Ms. Jackson?" The woman's accent was a strange combination of Midwestern with a hint of French. "My name is Sarah Mathews. My brother, Michael, asked me to contact you."

I was stunned for about three seconds, and then said, "Yes. I need to speak with you about your husband, Cal Bridgeton."

"He's no longer my husband, as least not according to the police, the insurance companies, or anyone else who matters."

"I understand that, but right now it's really important that you not be dead."

"Why's that?"

"Didn't your brother tell you?"

"Tell me what?"

"Cal Bridgeton is a suspect in another woman's murder." She was so quiet I thought she'd hung up. "Ms. Mathews?"

"Who?"

"Kristi Briggs. Does that name mean anything to you?"

"No, but I assume she's one of his women."

"You knew about his affairs?"

"Yes, each and every one, including when he began sleeping with my sister."

I didn't know what to say to that, so I took the conversation a different direction.

"My client, James Keeney, is being charged with your murder. You need to come back and speak with his public defender. They need to know what really happened that night. You told Michael that you weren't home, but..."

"I wasn't. I always went for a walk. That night, I left a little later than usual and forgot to grab my water bottle. That's why I stopped in the store. I'd actually never gone inside before."

If that was true, it could explain why she lingered inside.

"Ms. Jackson, I didn't have anything to do with Michelle's death, but I do have plenty of reason to believe I was Cal's intended victim that night. That's why I didn't come forward. If I return..."

"I can arrange protection for you. You'd be guarded twenty-four-seven by agents from Tracer International. Are you familiar with Tracer?"

"Yes, my parents used Tracer for several functions throughout the years."

"Then you also know their reputation. Your ex doesn't have any reason to believe that you're alive, right?"

"I don't think so."

"Then you don't have much to worry about. Fly into Lincoln. I'll meet you at the airport with two of Tracer's agents and we'll escort you to see Keeney's public defender. You'll give her a statement."

"But won't she need me to stay?"

"I don't know how long she might need you to stick around, but if you're concerned that Bridgeton would find out, then I'll arrange for you to stay in one of Tracer's safe houses."

There was a long pause before she finally spoke. "All right. How will I know who to look for?"

"I'll send you my picture after we hang up."

"Okay, give me an hour to schedule a flight."

"Ms. Mathews?"

"Yes?"

"I thought convincing you would be much more difficult."

"I'm not heartless, Ms. Jackson. Mr. Keeney shouldn't be punished for what Cal did. I was fine knowing he got away with it because I got away."

"But weren't you angry about what he did to Michelle?"

"Of course, but there wasn't anything I could do about that, and I feared that he'd find a way to get me, even if he got caught. He knows people."

"What kind of people?"

"The kind who don't mind killing."

SARAH MATHEW'S FLIGHT was scheduled to land at the Lincoln Airport at seven thirty in the evening. Specialists Bick and Leeds met me at her gate. Charlie agreed to fly with her, unbeknownst to her. A tall woman with shoulder-length blonde hair, pulling a small travel bag, entered the waiting area, followed by three other passengers, and then Charlie. He smiled and gave me a little tip of his Fedora hat when I saw him. He continued past us to the lounge.

"Ms. Mathews, I'm Dezeray Jackson. These are my associates, Specialist Bick," I gestured to a man with a medium build, bald head, and well-tanned skin from his recent travels to the Mid-East. "And this is Specialist Leeds." Leeds six-foot frame was well-muscled and dark. He always reminded me of Idris Elba minus the sexy accent. "Keeney's public defender agreed to meet with us at Tracer International headquarters. Bick and Leeds will take you. I need to follow-up with someone on a separate matter but will meet you there."

The specialists led Ms. Mathews out of the airport while I headed toward the bar. Charlie sat at the far end sipping something dark over ice, and people-watching. I strolled over, pulled out the chair next to his and sat.

"It's good to see you, Charlie."

He raised his glass and smiled. His hazel eyes sparkled, and his dimples were deeply set. "You too, Dez." Charlie could be mistaken for Cuban, Puerto Rican, Dominican, Arab – almost any light-skinned person, but he is biracial - black and white, like me. When people saw us together, they thought we were brother and sister. And that's pretty much the way we saw it, too.

"Any problems?" I asked.

"Nope. No one's tailing her from New Orleans."

"Thanks for hopping the flight at the last minute."

"No worries, you know that. Anything for you." He winked and sipped his drink.

"You headed straight back?"

"Have to. That Beautemps character keeps slipping past me. It's getting on my last nerve."

I stood to leave. "All right, then I better let you get back to it. Thanks, again, for keeping tabs on her." We did our usual fist-bump good-bye.

Fifteen minutes later I entered the lobby conference room at Tracer International. Keeney's public defender, Leeds, Bick and Sarah Mathews were all seated around the conference table engaged in idle chitchat.

"I'm sorry to have kept you waiting," I said, closing the door behind me. I took a seat next to Sarah. She smiled nervously at me. "I'm sure PD Clark has filled you in on James Keeney's situation, so why don't we get started?"

Marissa Clark opened a file, and removed crime-scene photos from the night Michelle was killed. Next to these she displayed pictures from journal entries and the fingerprint analysis that I'd provided to her from Charlie.

"Ms. Mathews, I will need confirmation that these prints belong to you."

"Of course, I understand."

"Are these your journals?"

Sarah nodded.

"And does this also belong to you?" PD Clark set the journal Keeney had found onto the table in front of us.

Again, Sarah nodded.

"If you knew that your husband was cheating on you, why didn't you just divorce him?" PD Clark asked. Putting witnesses on the defense came naturally to her, so I waited to hear Sarah's response.

"I intended to do exactly that."

"Why didn't you?"

"Because I saw him kill my sister."

My head jerked in her direction. "What?"

"I saw him kill Michelle," she repeated.

"Oh, shit. This isn't good," I said, looking across the table at PD Clark.

"Did Mr. Bridgeton know that you witnessed him killing Michelle?" Clark asked.

She shook her head. "I'd just returned home from my walk, and I heard some strange noise coming from the living room. I started to walk in, but I saw Cal standing behind someone. He had his right arm around her neck and was lifting her off the ground. I recognized the shoes. Michelle and I picked them out together."

"Why didn't you stop him?" PD Clark asked.

"I panicked. My office was close by, so I hid there until he left."

"He left?"

"Yes. And then a short time after that, I don't really know how long, the man you call James Keeney must have broken in. I didn't see him until he came into my office looking for my journals. I'd grabbed all, but one, and was about to leave. I had to wait for Keeney to get out of my office."

"Did you know that your husband had returned by then?"

"No. All I wanted to do was get my journals and some money I kept in a safe in my office."

"Did your husband know about the safe?" I asked.

"No, I don't think so. I had it installed after we were married, and I discovered his first little fling."

"Why?"

"I don't know. I guess I just wanted some cash on hand if I decided to leave."

"You knew he was cheating on you for most of your marriage. Why didn't you leave sooner?"

"Apparently, Ms. Clark, you're not married."

Marissa Clark squared her shoulders, ready to strike.

"I was ready to forgive Cal if it was a one-time thing. Why throw away our marriage for a fling? But then I realized it was more than that. He had a problem."

"Your father caught him," I said.

"I know. Cal was screwing Kristi Briggs and someone at his office. It wasn't the first time, so I wasn't shocked."

"Did your father tell you?"

"Not in so many words, but yes."

"How did you get out of the house without your husband or the police discovering you?" PD Clark asked.

"Cal didn't call the police right away. I could hear him pacing and talking to himself in the living room. He knew that he'd killed Michelle and not me, but he had no idea where I was. My office faces a garden on the south side of our house. I climbed out of one of the windows and ran. By the time I reached the end of the next block, I heard sirens."

"What'd you do? Where'd you go?" I asked.

"I called Michael. He picked me up, took me to his place, and I told him everything that happened. We decided that I should pretend to be Michelle."

"So he's known from the beginning?" I asked.

She nodded.

"Marissa, you have everything you need to get Keeney cleared of this, and then some."

"It looks that way." Marissa gathered all her papers and photos. "I need you to remain in Lincoln for now."

"How long?" Sarah asked.

"I'll see if I can get a meeting with the states attorney in the morning. He'll want to talk with you. Then, we'll just have to wait and see. From what I understand, Ms. Jackson's firm has a place for you to stay."

After PD Clark left, we escorted Sarah Mathews to one of Tracer's safe houses. It was in southwest Lincoln and hadn't been used for months. Bick and Leeds conducted the usual checks before I led Sarah into the house. The living and dining areas were open to the kitchen. She left her bag near the couch.

"Make yourself comfortable. The refrigerator is stocked if you're hungry. It's just the basics. You're going to need to stay inside. Don't answer the door. Don't sit on the back porch with your feet up."

She raised a hand to stop me. "I understand."

"I hope you do because it occurred to me while we were driving over here that you took a big risk."

"That's just now occurring to you?" She walked into the kitchen, found a glass, and filled it with water.

"I'm not talking about this." She was a smart-ass when what I was hoping for was smart. "You went to see your husband before leaving Omaha. Why did you do that?"

She turned back toward me and asked, "How?"

"Never mind that. Why did you take that risk?"

"I had to be sure he believed I was dead." She set the glass on the counter. "It was stupid. I realized that later."

"How did he react?"

"I'm not sure what his relationship with Michelle was by then. I expected him to be needier, but he stayed behind his desk replaying the night he found me—her."

"Are you sure that's all he said?"

She sipped her water, thinking. "Yes. He did seem oddly calm. Before I left, he got up, walked me to the door, and hugged me."

"How was that odd?"

"It wasn't that exactly. When he let go, the expression on his face—I can't quite describe it. It was like he suddenly remembered something. He returned to his desk without saying anything else."

I left Sarah at the safe house, pondering our conversation as I drove to Haithem's former apartment building. Tracer had a vacant apartment that I could use for the night. Inside the building, I waited for the elevator to descend. The doors opened and Steve Cochran stepped out.

"Here to break in, again?"

"Maybe. You have anything worth seeing?" I smiled, entered the elevator, and let the doors close.

Cochran wasn't a bad guy, and I did enjoy toying with him, but I was too tired to banter tonight. I'd let him stew over my comment for a while. My phone rang as I exited onto the fifth floor. It was Haithem.

"Where are you?" I asked, unlocking the apartment door while trying to hold the phone between my ear and shoulder.

"Still at Murphy's. Look, we can't talk long. I found the information you wanted about Savannah's killer."

I almost dropped the phone. I shoved the door closed with my foot, turned on a lamp, and asked, "Who?"

I GOT ABOUT THREE HOURS of solid sleep after my call from Haithem. Seventeen years of not knowing who killed my sister and I finally had his name. I knew exactly who he was, his backstory, everything except his current location. Haithem confirmed that the guy was ex-military, but that he'd been dishonorably discharged before completing his first four years. I wasn't clear how Senator Richie found him, but for now, that wasn't important to me.

After a quick shower to wake up, a strong cup of breakfast tea, and a toasted onion bagel smothered in cream cheese, I was ready to tackle the day. The breakfast was standard fair in Tracer apartments, along with fruit. An on-call housekeeper kept the apartments stocked. When I'd made arrangements the night before, she had everything I would need ready and waiting before I arrived.

As I drove to the states attorney's office, I reflected over everything I knew about Senator Richie, which wasn't a lot. Clearly, the man was insane. Maybe not clinically, but he was definitely screwed up. I had no idea the number of people he was responsible for killing throughout the years, but I did know that my family, Murphy, Haithem, and now Scott, were on his hit list. And that pissed me off. He was accustomed to using fear and intimidation, neither of which worked on me. Sometimes people imagine what it would be like to get revenge on the person they hate most. I don't imagine it; I do it. Maybe the senator and I have more in common than I thought.

Exiting the elevator, I saw Sarah, Leeds, Bick, and PD Clark waiting in the hallway. Lines etched across Marissa Clark's forehead as she spoke to Sarah.

"What's the hold up?" I asked, as I approached everyone. "The meeting was supposed to begin ten minutes ago."

"I'm not sure," Marissa said. "Assistant DA Stein is meeting with someone about that case in Omaha against Detrick Dixon. He's a man I hope to never meet."

"He's a kitten." I smiled.

She stared at me; head tilted slightly to the right. "Come again?"

"Just adding a bit of levity to the situation. Detrick Dixon isn't called Mad Dog for nothing, but you'll never cross paths with him. Public defenders aren't his style."

"Thankfully," she said, as a receptionist stepped into the hall to let us know that the Assistant DA was ready to see us.

Sarah whispered, "Who's Detrick Dixon?"

"No one you need to worry about. Totally different issue."

She nodded, and I followed her into the main office, after which the receptionist led us into a small conference room. Before long, Assistant DA Stein entered the room and Marissa Clark spent the next fifteen minutes detailing her findings.

"Based on what we're telling you, there's no grounds to charge James Keeney with the murder of Sarah Bridgeton or Michelle Mathews," Clark said.

"I'll need to discuss the case with the Omaha District Attorney's office before I'd be willing to drop the charges. You've presented me with a witness, but I'll need to investigate what Mrs. Bridgeton has told me. Until I do, Mr. Keeney is still our guy, and he's definitely on the hook for another B&E. Mrs. Bridgeton, you're going to need to stick around a little longer so we can dot some i's and cross some t's."

Sarah nodded and said, "I understand. I just want to help Mr. Keeney and see that my husband is punished for what he did to Michelle."

"OPD still is interested in your husband for the Briggs' death."

It was fleeting, but I could have sworn Sarah smiled. It was sort of a quick, crooked grin. I dismissed it as relief. She'd been through a lot in the past twenty-four hours.

"For now, let's make sure Mrs. Bridgeton is secure," Stein said. "I'll be in touch." He stood, signaling the end of our meeting; we left the district attorney's office.

SARAH BRIDGETON WAS in good hands, so I felt comfortable returning to Omaha to check on Godfrey. The poor dog had been left outside all night. Luckily for my neighbors, and me, he wasn't a barker; he preferred the sneak attack to alerting.

Godfrey, excited to see me, knocked over his water dish as he ran inside. The water spread across the floor and beneath the table. Grabbing a towel, I got down on all fours to clean up the mess, when something under the tabletop caught my eye. It was another bugging device. Either we missed it the first time, or the asshole got into my house again. I snatched it from its hiding spot, walked outside, and attached it to a tree. Then I went back inside to get my bow.

Before lining up for the shot, I whispered into the bug, "Come out, come out, wherever you are." I stepped back several feet, aimed, and nailed it dead center. I took a long, satisfying breath, removed my arrow from the tree, and returned to the house. A Post-It note that I hadn't noticed earlier, was stuck to the door of the microwave. It was from Murphy telling me that Scott had Remington in his sights and Murphy was on his way to meet Haithem. When Scott and Tango had Remington, they planned to meet back up with Murphy and Haithem. He didn't say where, and I didn't want to know.

I checked the house for more bugs. There weren't any, so that made me think we missed the one I'd just found, not that it mattered. The result was the same. Richie was sicking his dog on me, and I planned to find it and put it down. I'd let Murphy and Haithem handle the senator. I still hadn't told my father anything I'd discovered the past several months. That conversation was overdue, and I dreaded having it.

Back in my office I dialed his personal cell number. I knew he'd be at the office, but this way, he could walk away from whoever might be around him. He answered on the first ring.

"Dez?" We hadn't spoken in a month, mainly because of his schedule. He'd gone overseas to assist a client.

"We need to talk."

"Okay." I heard him close a door. "What's going on?"

"I know what happened to Savannah and to mom. I also know who did it."

I spent the next hour filling him in on the details. My father was a calm man. Years of military training had taught him patience and the importance of timing.

"What do you need from me?"

"Haithem plans to leak information about the senator to his international media contacts. That'll start the ball rolling. I just wanted to give you a heads-up."

"And the Covington issue?"

"It's not an issue anymore. Scott James is the only one left." I decided that he didn't need to know about Remington. Not now. I also didn't mention that I had the name of Savannah's killer. If I'd told him, he would have ordered me to step off, and I had no intention of doing that. Dealing with the senator was a delicate proposition. Taking Savannah and my mother's killer to task was a whole other thing. I wanted to see the senator rot in prison. That wasn't my plan for the man he hired.

"Senator Richie will pay for what he did, Dad."

"You're right, he will, but you need to promise me that you'll let Haithem take care of things."

"Of course. What? You think I'd go after the senator?"

"We're both angry, but this situation calls for level-headed thinking."

"I can be level-headed."

"Not where your sister and mother are concerned. Promise me."

"I promise not to go after the senator." My father had no idea that the senator still had someone coming after me and my promise didn't include him. "But Dad, you need to put shadows around Luke and Troy."

"That's already done. It occurred to me while you were receiving those strange messages from Covington that maybe it wouldn't hurt to get a few eyes on your brothers." There was a brief pause, then, "Dez, watch your six."

"I am, Dad. Don't worry. Murphy's never too far, and of course, there's always Eddy." Eddy and my dad were old friends. "And if I get desperate, I'll get in touch with Katrina."

"You two still on the outs?"

"Things are complicated."

My father knew that Katrina lived on the wrong side of things, but he considered her one of the family. Truth was, so did I, and I always would.

CHAPTER ELEVEN

"KATRINA, I NEED YOU to do something for me."

Katrina leaned into the couch and crossed her legs. I'd decided to meet her at Easy Street before it opened at five o'clock. Coming any later would have been a distraction for both of us. The company she kept at her club always negatively affected her attitude.

"Last time you came at me, you threatened to give me a beatdown." That was true. She'd pushed me on the whole Clive and Detrick situation.

"You know I didn't mean it."

"It sounded like you meant it."

Now she was toying with me.

"Okay, fine. You want me to say it, I'll say it."

She drummed her fingers on the arm of the couch, grinning.

"I'm sorry I threatened you."

"See how easy that was?"

I sat in one of the lounge chairs across from her.

"Since we're on the topic, what's Detrick's status?"

"The lawyers are handling that."

"You don't seem concerned."

"Detrick's been running these streets for as long as I've been the Queen. He's not going anywhere. And you can stop worrying about Clive. I don't have any plans for him." She reached for a glass of water that a server had just delivered. "What do you need?"

"Someone's following me, and I don't have time right now to deal with him."

"You know it's a *him*?"

"Yes, but I don't have much more than that. He planted three bugs in my house and tried to mess with my Jeep."

"Mess with your Jeep?"

"It looks like he might have been trying to make it go boom." I gestured an explosion for emphasis.

"You're making all kinds of new friends since you got back."

"Looks like."

"What do you want me to do?"

"I need a few people to have my back. Be my eyes."

"Protection? Christ, Dez, you work for Tracer International. They could do it."

"I have a feeling that this particular guy would see them. And this is a personal issue."

"Personal?" Her nails tapped on the side of her glass. "Is this about Savannah?"

"Yes."

"Is he the guy?"

"No, I don't think so."

"Then who is he?"

"Someone hired him to kill me."

Katrina's fingers stopped tapping.

"Who?"

"I can't tell you that, yet."

"But you do know?"

I nodded.

"Okay, I have a few guys I can send your way. Do you want to meet them?"

"No, I think it's better if I don't. I don't want my admirer connecting the dots. Anytime they notice a white male in my general vicinity, tell them to snap a picture. He's got an average build and was in the military, but I don't know how skilled he is."

"They'll be discreet. That's what I pay them for."

I stood to leave. "Thanks, Katrina."

Katrina stood, setting her glass on the table. She was several inches taller than me and could have been a model. Her long blond hair was pulled into a low ponytail. She wore a deep-purple cocktail dress covered with sequins. Even in it, she intimidated everyone within twenty feet of her with a simple glance in their direction. I'd known her long before she created this persona and helped her develop "the look" as a defensive technique.

The day we met she was being chased by a group of girls from our school. It was raining the day she stumbled into my parents' dojang soaked and crying. We got her cleaned up and from that day we became best friends. Eventually, she earned her first-degree black belt in Hapkido from my father, then she stopped training when I left to attend the University of Nebraska-Lincoln. During one of my trips home, I found out she was dealing.

"Dez, they'll be armed."

"I know."

"If this guy gets within range, they'll take him out."

"Only if he's close and I don't see him. I don't want him dead."

"I'll tell my guys."

I turned to walk away.

"Be alert," she said.

"Always." I gave her a backhanded wave and descended the spiral stairs to the main floor.

FROM EASY STREET, I drove to The Lab to talk with Dawn Ryker. I'd dropped off the photos of my admirer earlier in the week. She'd sent me a text before I stopped to see Katrina.

I walked the long, narrow, white-walled corridor to the observation area above the main labs, where I was pretty confident I'd find Dr. Ryker. She was where I expected, inside her lab conducting chemistry experiments. At least that's the way it always looked to me. I had no clue what the woman really did. I did know that she excelled at it, though. Slackers don't make it through Tracer's hiring process. She looked up, saw me, and pointed to her watch. While I waited, I observed a few other scientists who busied themselves in labs near hers. One was reviewing a body. Another looked like he was putting together a bomb. I checked my watch.

After about five minutes, Dawn Ryker emerged from her lab carrying a manila folder and met me at the top of the stairs above the lab rooms. I followed her into one of the small, glass-walled conference rooms near the observation area. She closed the door behind me, and we sat at the table.

"We were able to enhance the images a little, but you still can't make out his face at all. In one of the pictures..." She shuffled through the small pile. "Here it is. You see that?" She pointed to something that looked like a cross on the inside of the man's wrist just above his glove. "That's a tattoo of a Maltese cross."

"I've seen this before."

"Where?"

"Someone else's wrist."

"This cross has an interesting history. Its origins date back to sixteenth-century Malta and the Knights of Malta. You can see that there are eight points."

I nodded.

"Each point symbolizes the obligations or aspirations of the knights."

"Like what?"

"Truth, faith, repentance, humility, justice, mercy, sincerity, and to endure persecution."

I stared at her, amazed that she could just rattle that off.

"I'm a history buff." She smiled. "Maybe this guy is somehow associated with the person you saw before."

"Maybe."

"I found another interesting tidbit of information about this cross. It's the symbol for the United States Marine Corps Sharpshooter Badge. Isn't that fascinating? I mean, a symbol that represents all those positive attributes used to represent the ability to kill at a distance? The irony." She shook her head.

"The Marine Corps? Are you sure?"

"Oh, yes. Absolutely."

"Dawn, you're a genius!"

"Well, I don't know about that." Her face flushed.

I stood, gathered the pictures, and slid them back inside the folder.

"I hope this helps. Let me know if you need anything else." She stood and opened the door.

"I will. Thanks!"

Back inside the comfort of my Jeep, I called the number Murphy had given me to keep in touch. A minute later he called back.

"Covington, the one at the Coffee Nut had a tattoo on the inside of his wrist of a Maltese Cross. Guess who else has the same tattoo?"

"Who?"

"My new admirer and Scott."

"Really?"

"Yep. And you know what that symbol means in the Marine Corps?"

"Sharpshooter." Murphy had the badge, but not the tattoo. "I wouldn't have pegged James as a sharpshooter."

"Stay focused, Murphy. That's not what's important. What if his entire unit had these tattoos? Maybe my new admirer was a member of their original team."

"There were only five."

"Five that we know about."

"There's only one person who can confirm this for you."

"Have you been in touch with him?"

"I'll reach out to Tango. See where they are."

The call ended. It was past seven o'clock and I didn't have any more leads to follow. I started the Jeep, pulled into traffic, and contemplated what I'd have for dinner. Cooking for one didn't appeal to me and being around a crowd of people appealed to me even less, but I needed to eat. I checked my side mirror and noticed that I'd picked up a tail a few cars back. Maneuvering my Jeep, I could just make out two black guys wearing ball caps. That's all the detail I wanted. Katrina was on point.

As I drove west on Dodge Road, the familiar pull to have a Guinness tugged at me, so I stopped at Brazen Head. Mick was tending bar when I stepped through the entrance. He had my beer poured, and set, before I pulled out a seat and removed my jacket. It was a slow night with only a few tables occupied.

"You send those flowers and tickets to Cynthia yet?" I asked.

"Yes, I did."

I loved hearing his Irish accent. "And?"

"We're planning to get together."

"Told ya."

Mick grinned, as he filled a glass for a new customer who'd just sat at the bar a few chairs from me. He was wearing a knit hat, black leather jacket, blue jeans, and looked like he hadn't shaved in days. He didn't remove his sunglasses, which I thought was more than a little strange. I ordered my usual boxty and watched a soccer game on the TV. After a few hours, I had my fill of food and Guinness, paid my tab, and said goodnight to Mick.

"I'll let you know how it goes," Mick said, as he began clearing my dishes and cleaning the space.

"Oh, I'm sure I'll find out before I see you next." I waved as I exited the restaurant.

The man who'd been sitting at the bar stood to follow me out. Normally, I'd think this was a coincidence. Katrina's guys had parked several spaces away from my Jeep. I couldn't see them, but I nodded in their direction. The driver flashed his high beams, then shut them off. I heard the door to Brazen Head open, then close as I walked to my Jeep. Making a point not to look over my shoulder, I kept an eye on Katrina's men. One had gotten out of the car and started walking toward Brazen Head. He must have bumped into the guy because I heard someone with a deep voice say, "Excuse me, brother. Sorry about that." The other man said, "Don't worry about it." Then it sounded like someone was walking away from me. I climbed inside my Jeep, started the engine, and flipped on my lights. The man was gone, and Katrina's guy was heading back to his car.

"MR. BRIDGETON?" I STOOD at the entrance of my front door looking out at Cal Bridgeton through the storm door. He was dressed in casual slacks, a polo shirt, and navy jacket. "It's seven in the morning. Why are you at my house? Wait. How did you know where I lived?"

"Are you going to let me inside? I mean I'd rather not have this conversation out here."

"Hang on." I closed and locked the door. I'd gotten up late and still wasn't dressed. Godfrey followed me back upstairs. He was about as awake as I was. I brushed my teeth, tossed my curls around to loosen them up, and spritzed them with a little water and leave-in conditioner to soften them. Today was a jeans and T-shirt kind of day, with my favorite shit-kickers. Five minutes later, I opened the door and invited Cal Bridgeton into my home.

"Is there something I can help you with?" I didn't invite him to sit. We stood in the entryway.

"I need your help. This might seem strange, me coming to you, but you're the only private investigator that I know. And I don't have the luxury of researching anyone else's qualifications."

"Mr. Bridgeton, I think there might be a conflict of interest here."

He raised both of his hands in front of him to stop me from continuing. "Just hear me out."

I gestured to the couch, inviting him to sit, and I sat to his left in my oversized chair. Godfrey came into the living room and positioned himself between us.

"Nice dog."

"Not really. Why are you here?"

"Sarah isn't dead." I could tell by his expression that he expected me to be surprised.

"What makes you say that?"

"When I arrived home that night, I believed I'd found her. She wasn't dead and I fumbled to get the phone, but then I heard a noise. When I went to check it out, I didn't find anyone. I know now that it was probably Keeney. By the time I returned to Sarah, she was dead."

"That's why there was a delay between the time you found the body and when you called nine-one-one?"

"Yes."

"Why don't you believe Sarah is dead? What changed your mind?"

"She came to my office before the funeral. It was sort of surreal. I hadn't seen Michelle for weeks. When she walked into my office, I was confused."

"Why?"

"Her walk was different. Michelle had a strut that radiated confidence. It was who she was. You know how some women raise the temperature of a room when they enter it?"

I nodded.

"That was Michelle. Sarah was never like that."

"Okay, but her sister had just been murdered."

"Before she said good-bye, I embraced her and noticed that she didn't smell like Michelle."

This was a new one.

"Excuse me?" I asked.

"Michelle always wore Chanel Number Five. It was her signature perfume. Every holiday, every birthday, I bought it for her, even when we weren't together."

"Your argument for Sarah being alive rests on a strut and perfume."

"I know it sounds crazy, but now someone is trying to frame me for murdering Kristi Briggs. If the police push forward, then my lawyers believe they'll reexamine Sarah's case."

"Why haven't you told the police about Sarah?"

"I don't know where she is, and they wouldn't believe me. It'd be like a bad remake of The Fugitive." He leaned forward, stroking his neck, causing Godfrey to growl at his sudden movement. Bridgeton sat back with his hands on his lap.

"Godfrey doesn't appreciate sudden moves from strangers in his house."

"I see that."

"If I believe you, and Sarah is alive, why wouldn't she have come forward?"

"Because she killed Michelle. It's the only thing that makes any sense to me."

"I thought you believed it was James Keeney?"

"I wanted to believe that, but when Kristi was killed, I knew it couldn't have been."

"There might not even be a connection between the two cases."

"The common denominator is me. I know that and the police know that, but I didn't kill either of them." Godfrey's low rumble forced Bridgeton to calm his tone. "Look, I wasn't the greatest husband. I think you know that by now. I thought maybe Sarah decided to just leave. Thinking about it now, I realize how naive that sounds. It's more likely that she was trying to frame me for Michelle's murder."

Maybe, I thought. It was a possibility.

"Okay, let's say that I'm willing to entertain your story. What do you expect me to do?"

"Help me prove she's alive. The police can take it from there. Sarah would have to explain why she left and where she's been all this time. My attorneys said that finding her would give the police another suspect."

"Why would she come back just to frame you? She's been away for a few years. She supposedly has a new life."

"You're underestimating how much she hates me. You've been right about me so far, Ms. Jackson. Sarah knew about my affairs. She confronted me a few weeks before Michelle was killed. My attorneys want me to tell the police the truth about our relationship. I didn't before because I didn't want to embarrass her family."

"Mr. Bridgeton, I'll see what I can find out about Sarah's whereabouts. If I discover anything that will help you, I'll be in touch." I stood, expecting him to do the same. He didn't.

"Thank you," he said, looking up at me. Godfrey stood and began growling.

"He's telling you that it's time for you to leave. You should probably listen."

Bridgeton got up and walked to the door. Before opening it, he said, "The police told me that Kristi was strangled. They think we were having 'rough sex' and things got out of hand. We're addicts, but we weren't into that sort of thing."

"I'll check things out."

"DALTON, I THINK WE have a problem."

"What's that Ms. Jackson?"

"Were you able to account for Sarah Bridgeton's whereabouts from the time before Michelle's funeral until her arrival in Lincoln a few days ago?"

I was sitting in Haithem's Lincoln office sifting through a file of information I'd gathered on Keeney's case, so far. Dalton sat in a chair on the other side of the desk reviewing his notes.

"France, Buenos Aires." He was ticking the places off with his fingers. "Back to France, then New York City, back to France, then New York City, again, and finally, New Orleans. All of the dates flow—wait a minute."

I looked up. "What is it?"

"She arrived in New Orleans, but she didn't travel from New York City to New Orleans. I didn't find any flight schedule for that. I don't know how she got to New Orleans."

"All right, that's something to check into. Look for train and bus routes first, then check car rentals. See if she made any stops along the way."

"I'm on it." Dalton disappeared to do his research magic.

I CHECKED IN WITH BICK and Leeds to make sure Sarah was still where she needed to be, and then I headed to the public defender's office. Everything Cal Bridgeton told me was plausible and that bothered me. I hadn't completely ruled Sarah Bridgeton out, but I was ready to believe her over her ex-husband. I just couldn't get my head around the idea that she would kill her sister over an affair with her husband. It was the whole 'blood is thicker than water' thing. I'd have expected her to ruin him through divorce like a normal rich person would do. My bullshit meter was running high, but I had to do my due diligence—dot all the i's and cross all the t's. Isn't that what Assistant DA Stein had said?

Marissa Clark sat across from me behind her small desk. I'd just started filling her in on my chat with Cal Bridgeton when there was a knock on her office door.

"Marissa, you might want to tune in to channel six."

She turned on a TV mounted to a wall in the corner of her office, behind the door. I rotated my chair so I could see.

Cal Bridgeton, partner at Bridgeton & Myers Engineering firm, has been arrested in connection with the murder of Kristi Briggs. Mr. Bridgeton's lawyers would not comment on their client's arrest except to say that their client would be found innocent. His partner, Sam Myers, also wasn't available for comment.

Marissa turned the TV off.

"That's an interesting development," she said. "If they're charging him, they must have something solid connecting him to Briggs. And they'll probably be more willing to reopen their investigation in the Mathews' case to see if he's good for that, too. Things are beginning to look pretty good for James Keeney right now."

"True, and that's who's paying me, but what if Cal Bridgeton didn't do any of this."

"You really think Sarah Bridgeton is lying?"

"I'm saying that it's possible."

The ring from my phone interrupted our conversation.

"I'm sorry, but I have to take this." I stepped out of her office, "Hold on," I said to Murphy as I walked down the hall, past the reception area, and into the lobby. "Okay, go ahead."

"We've got Remington. That Maltese Cross tattoo was something their crew did together. All of them received their sharpshooter badges around the same time. So, there were originally six. James said that they believed their sixth, a guy named Greg Mitchel, was killed during a mission they'd completed for Commander Earley. Haithem's searching for details about Mitchel now, but it looks like he's your new admirer."

"Now that we know who he is, he should be easier to deal with," I said.

"He's not just a sharpshooter. Apparently, he was their munitions expert."

"That would explain him going for my Jeep."

"Yep, but keep in mind that he's got the same general training as your boy, James. He's dangerous with a capital D and I can't stick around to help you deal with him. We've got to handle Remington and the senator."

"Don't worry about me, I called in a little backup."

"You told your father?"

"No, not exactly, but he reminded me that I have a few people around me who I can count on in a pinch."

"Eddy?"

"No, Katrina."

"Good luck with that."

"She's got two guys watching my back, and last night it came in handy."

"What happened last night?"

"Nothing, that's the point."

"I'll get back in touch before we move on the senator. Tell your dad to keep watching CNN."

"Will do."

I returned to Marissa Clark's office to pick up where we'd left off. She was on her way out as I walked in.

"I was just coming to look for you. Assistant DA Stein gave Sarah Bridgeton's statement to the Omaha DA. He wants to meet with her this afternoon."

"I'll take her. Will you be there?"

"Yes. This still involves my client. Stein will also be there."

"What time?"

"Can you get her there by three o'clock?"

"That should be fine. I'll head over to the safe house now."

"MS. JACKSON, I SAW that Cal was arrested." Sarah Bridgeton was getting settled in my Jeep. I started the engine and the radio blared reggae beats. I hit the dial to turn it off.

"Yes, I saw that, too."

"So this must mean that they have enough evidence. Maybe they don't need me to stay?"

"That's not my decision."

"You've got experience with this, though. Do you think I'll have to see him?"

"Not initially, but at some point, you might be called to testify."

"What could I possibly testify about? I didn't know the woman."

"You could testify about your relationship. Your sexual relationship. The DA will want to show that your ex-husband had a history of engaging in certain types of sexual behaviors."

"I don't think I could do that."

"His attorneys also might want to talk with you, but to show that he didn't engage in deviant sex acts. I'm speculating, Sarah. I really don't know."

We continued to Omaha in silence for another thirty minutes. Then she started talking.

"Maybe he did those things with Michelle, but never with me."

In my experience, when someone leads with something like that, it's best to let them keep going, so I did the appropriate nod and sounds of encouragement, letting her know that I was listening.

"When I learned about all his affairs, I was angry. I mean what woman wouldn't be? And then he told me he was a sex addict. Seriously? Christ, it was just an excuse to make him feel better about fucking all those women."

"Uh, huh."

"But my sister? He couldn't keep it in his pants around my sister? I supposed it was every man's fantasy."

I glanced at her.

"Twins."

"Oh," I said.

"Michelle and I were so different. She was wild and had to be the center of attention. Do you know what she did at our wedding?"

I raised my eyebrows.

"Not only did she screw the best man, who was married to one of my closest friends, by the way, but I walked in on her giving Sam Myers a blow job in my bridal suite."

That got my attention. I didn't realize Sam Myers and Michelle got together that soon.

"I thought Myers and your sister dated at some point."

"Dated? Michelle didn't date men, she fucked men, especially married men."

"You seem angrier at her than at your husband."

She sighed deeply. "I'm not angry at her anymore. I let that go."

"When?"

"What?"

"When did you let your anger go?" We'd arrived in Omaha, and I followed Interstate 680 downtown.

"I don't know. It just got easier the longer I was away." She was calm, again. "I'm looking forward to leaving."

"The fact that you're alive and Michelle is dead is going to bring a lot of attention your way."

"I know and I'm hoping I won't be forced to stay in Omaha and endure it. Cal deserves the attention. I don't."

"But there's bound to be confusion about why you left. Why you didn't tell the police that it was your sister who died."

"I think a lot of people want a fresh start. I was given one and I took it. It was Michelle's gift to me."

That was an interesting choice of words. I pulled into a parking garage, and we walked to the DA's office. A few reporters were camped out in front of the office when we stepped out of the elevator. One shouted, "Ms. Bridgeton! It's Michelle Bridgeton."

She smiled politely and kept walking. I grabbed her elbow, leading her into the office. The receptionist directed us to a large conference room where Stein, Clark, and DA Brown waited.

For the next hour, DA Brown interviewed Sarah Bridgeton, trying to determine her involvement in the past and current case. When he finished his questions, Sarah asked, "Am I free to leave? I'd like to return to New Orleans. I'm sure you can appreciate my desire to get as far from this media circus as possible."

"Of course, Mrs. Bridgeton. We'll bring you back during the trial phase. Thank you for your statement."

With that, the meeting ended, and I drove Sarah Bridgeton back to Lincoln to retrieve her things. She arranged for a flight to New Orleans as we drove. The rest of the time, we sat in an uncomfortable silence, but I couldn't put my finger on why?

CHAPTER TWELVE

"CHARLIE? THIS IS DEZ."

"How's that case you're working?"

"That's why I'm calling. Sarah Bridgeton is scheduled to return to New Orleans tonight around eleven thirty. Can you keep eyes on her for the next few days?" I had already dropped her at the airport and was headed back to Omaha.

"Sure, but why?"

"Something just doesn't feel right."

"You got a little Mayville Toussaint in your blood?"

"Maybe."

"I'll keep you informed."

"You get a bead on Cyrano Beautemps, yet?"

"Yeah, finally. Word is he's hiding out in the Quarter."

"Good luck."

"It ain't about luck, baby girl, it's about skill."

"True, but a little luck never hurt nobody."

"When your case is finished, you should come down for a visit. It's been a longtime since we hit up the jazz clubs."

"Sounds like a good plan. Let's make it happen, soon. I feel winter around the corner and I might need a nice warm place to relax."

"You know my mama's place is always open to you. She's been wondering where you been hiding. Didn't believe me when I said you went back to Omaha. Well, until I told her about the free house."

"Too good to pass up, that's for sure."

"You think you'll stay there long? I know we share that itch to bounce."

"I don't know. It's been a year and business is good. If I do leave, I'll keep the house. Maybe rent it out. And I've got Godfrey to think about now."

"Godfrey?"

"I adopted a Rottweiler."

"Oh, shit! You got all domesticated on me?"

"This is about as domesticated as I'll ever get."

"That's my girl. Listen, I need to be gettin to the airport if I'm gonna catch up with Sarah Bridgeton. Give Mama a call. She misses you."

The call disconnected and I turned on the radio. There was nothing but crap playing, so I grabbed my Queen Greatest Hits CD and jammed to *Another One Bites the Dust*. My mind wandered to the conversation Cal Bridgeton and I had about Michelle's perfume. Chanel Number Five. Her signature scent. Sarah must have known that about her sister. Why would she walk into his office pretending to be Michelle without wearing her sister's signature scent? Maybe her focus was on getting out of town and she simply forgot. Or maybe she wanted him to know that she was getting away from him. Either way, I couldn't let it go. I needed to talk to Cal Bridgeton, again. And it wouldn't hurt to touch base with Sam Myers. Did he know about Michelle's perfume? If he did, then Cal Bridgeton was telling the truth. At least about that. I was beginning to feel played. And I don't like that feeling. It pisses me off.

I pulled into my driveway and noticed Katrina's guys parked a half block east of my house. It was nice knowing that someone was watching my place, and I figured that they'd alert me if there was anything to worry about. They didn't, so I went inside. Godfrey turned in circles, and then darted to the kitchen.

A second later he sat in front of me with his food bowl dangling from his mouth. Feeding him is what I imagined feeding a horse would be like. I didn't buy the expensive dog food 'cause it would bankrupt me. I picked some middle-of-the-road variety I could buy at nearly any store. That was a good thing, too, because when I walked into the kitchen to feed him, I realized I was out of dog food. Shit.

"I'll be right back, Godfrey." I opened the refrigerator and found a bag of sliced Turkey. The sell-by date had passed a few days ago. It smelled a little off. "Here. I don't want it, that's for sure." Godfrey eats everything. I don't feed him the things that will kill him, but that doesn't stop him from begging for them. I made brownies once and he was convinced that I was holding out on him. He whined and howled. I put them in the oven for safekeeping. When I got back from a workout, the oven door was open, and Godfrey lay on the floor, a pile of vomit next to him. You'd think he'd learn, but he's not like us. When we toss our cookies, we avoid the thing we believed did us in. To this day, I can't stand the smell of Peach Schnapps, but when he smells chocolate, he begs for it.

I opened the front door and stood face to face with Clive Dixon.

"What the hell are you doing here?" I asked.

"Katrina sent me. Said you needed backup."

"She already sent a few guys."

"No, she didn't. Not yet."

"Then who the hell are the two guys in that car down the street?"

Clive looked over his shoulder not too discreetly and shrugged. "She's got a few people on their way but told me to come over and keep you company."

"Come inside." I backed up, allowing him to pass, and closed the door. "Who the hell are they? This makes no sense. When did Katrina talk to you?"

"The other day, when I was at Eddy's. She stopped in, told us about your little problem. Said she was lining things up but had to reallocate resources."

"Us?"

"Yeah, Eddy and me."

"Those are Eddy's guys?"

"Don't know."

I grabbed my phone to call Eddy.

"Eddy, this is Dez. Do you have two guys watching me?"

"No, why? What's going on?"

"Nothing. I'm just trying to figure something out."

"I can be there in five if you need me to be."

"No, everything's fine. Thanks." I hung up. "Those guys have been watching me since I first spoke to Katrina. Are you sure they don't work for her?"

"She planned to get a few dudes you've never seen around her. They're supposed to be here in the morning, but I don't know when."

I walked to the bay window and peeked out. They were still there. My mind reviewed everything I knew about when I first picked up the tail. They were staying back except for the other night. They stepped between me and my admirer, so they were here to help me. At least, that's what I hoped.

I LET CLIVE STAY ON the couch. By the time I walked upstairs, Godfrey was snoring on the floor in front of my bedroom door. I stepped over him and went around to the side of my bed to the nightstand. I opened the gun vault I'd mounted to the side, beneath the drawer, placed my gun inside, and closed the door. I'd picked up several of these from a recent trip to Costco and strategically placed them throughout the house. There was one in the bathroom, the kitchen, the basement, my office, and near my entryway table. I kept pistols in all but two. Those were reserved for the ones I carried.

Sleep was elusive and I tossed most of the night. Finally, around four-thirty, I got out of bed and cleaned up. Clive was asleep when I entered the living room. I checked outside to see that my guards were still there. A quiver moved down my spine as a cold draft entered through a dining-room window I didn't remember leaving open. The drapes swayed, and then settled. I walked over to shut it, inspecting it first. From what I could determine, no one had entered the house through it, but I removed my gun from my back holster and moved room to room just to be sure. Satisfied that I was alone, except for still sleeping Clive and snoring Godfrey, I started making breakfast and mentally organizing my day.

After breakfast, I retreated to the basement for a little knife-throwing practice. It'd been a few days since my last session. Thirty minutes later, I heard movement upstairs and the *click click* of Godfrey's toenails on the kitchen floor. He ambled halfway down the basement stairs and stared at me. I knew that look well. Rather than continue down the steps, he slowly backed himself up until he reached the top. Clive was in the kitchen with his head peering into the refrigerator.

"Got any orange juice?"

"Do you see any?"

"Nope."

"Then I don't have any."

"Why you so grumpy this morning?" he asked, taking a carton of eggs out and placing it on the counter next to the stove.

"I don't appreciate having unexpected guests. And the fact Katrina thought sending you was a good idea..."

"She didn't exactly send me."

Head tilted and eyebrows raised, I looked at Clive, waiting for an explanation.

"What happened was, she came into Eddy's like I said, and was talking to him about you. Since I'm sort of between places, I thought you could use the company." He smiled, cracked an egg, and put it into the pan. Then he cracked two more. "Got any bacon or sausages?"

"Did you see any?"

"You need to go shopping." He took two slices of bread from the bag on the counter and tossed them into the toaster. "No coffee either, huh?"

"I don't drink coffee."

"Oh, yeah. I forgot. You don't even know how to make it. Good thing your auntie left you a coffee maker, huh?"

Smartass.

"Eddy says I can work a few nights a week at the hall. You still need an assistant?"

"That depends."

"On what?"

"How annoying you are."

"You know you love me." He turned back to the stove, turned off the flame and slid his eggs onto his toast. I happened to have a few bananas and he took one before setting his plate onto the table. "I thought about what you said."

I wasn't sure what he was talking about, so I pulled out a chair and listened.

"I need to do something more with my life. Detrick never wanted me dealing, but I didn't know anything else. But I got skills, and like you said, they're transferable."

I didn't remember that conversation, but okay.

"I was thinkin you could train me how to do what you do."

It was true he had skills, and I knew with the right exposure, possibly even some training from Tracer, Clive had potential.

"If you're serious, then it's something I'd be willing to entertain. But Clive..." He looked up at me from his plate. "Don't waste my time. And you're not staying here. I'll help you get out of Detrick's place and into something you can afford that's not in the shits."

"That's cool, Ms. D. You're awright."

"Just eat. I've got things to do."

While Clive finished his breakfast, I went into my office to check messages and e-mail. One was from Charlie. It'd come in around two in the morning. I tapped in my security pin and played it.

"Dez, your girl never showed. I waited, thinking maybe she ended up on a different flight. She's in the wind."

Ah, shit. I knew something wasn't right. I grabbed my satchel from the entryway table and yelled for Clive to haul ass.

"Where we headed?"

"I've got a few people I need to talk to this morning. Where am I dropping you?"

"I'll come with you. Training, right?"

"Fine, but keep your mouth shut and listen."

SAM MYERS WAS IN HIS office when I knocked on the door. I'd told Clive to wait in the reception area, figuring that Daniel would enjoy the company. Myers had just hung up the phone when he saw me waiting. He waved me in and invited me to sit.

"Mr. Myers, I don't want to waste your time or mine, so I'm going to give you a rundown of what I already know."

He pushed away from his desk, leaned back in his high-back leather executive chair, and clasped his fingers in front of his stomach.

"I know about your sister, the Erwischt Holding Company, great name choice by the way, and that you had a relationship with Michelle that began on Cal Bridgeton's wedding day. I also get why you're going after Bridgeton. You want to see him ruined."

Myers scoffed. "Ruined? More like devastated."

"And I'm pretty certain you'll get your wish, but I don't believe he killed Michelle Mathews or Kristi Briggs."

"There's no one else who could have. He had opportunity and motive. At least that's what the district attorney believes." He smiled.

"Doesn't it bother you at all that your firm's name is associated with all that's happening?"

"You've done your research, so you also know that my objective was to buy him out, which as of a few hours ago, I've done. He'll be lucky if his lawyers continue representing him now that he has no way to pay them."

"You bought him out, so he has some funds."

"He and this firm were so leveraged that I was able to swoop in with my holding company to 'save it.'" He did the whole air-quotes thing. "The only thing Cal gets in the deal is his job, but not for long."

"What perfume did Michelle wear?"

"Perfume?"

I nodded.

"Chanel Number Five. It was her favorite. Why?"

"I just needed confirmation." I stood, turning toward the door to leave.

"Confirmation of what?"

I paused. Turning back to face him, I said, "Confirmation that Cal Bridgeton was telling the truth."

"About what?" He scooted forward, placing his hands in a steeple position on the desk.

"Sarah Bridgeton went to see Cal Bridgeton but was posing as Michelle. Michelle always wore Chanel Number Five. Sarah wasn't wearing any perfume."

"Are you saying that Sarah is alive?"

"Yes."

"Then he killed Michelle. It's that simple."

"No, it's not."

I left the office and discovered Daniel giving Clive phone-etiquette lessons.

"I'm done here. Let's go." Clive grabbed his jacket from a nearby sofa and pushed the button for the elevator. "Daniel, you might need to consider new employment."

"Why? What'd he tell you?" He raced from behind his desk and to the elevators. "Is Erwischt firing everyone?"

"You should talk to Myers and see what his plans are. Erwischt is his company."

"I knew it!" Daniel liked playing amateur sleuth. "He's been so secretive. And it's perfectly logical that he'd push Mr. Bridgeton out. I'm going to go talk with him right now."

We entered the elevator and Clive turned to me and said, "He's gay, right?"

"I believe so. Is there a problem?"

"No, no problem. I just wanted to be sure I was reading him right."

"You're going to meet some interesting people in this line of work. And you'll have to learn to go with the flow."

"I can do that."

We exited the elevator on the main floor. "Where we headed now?"

"I need to find someone."

"WHAT I'M TELLING YOU is that Cal Bridgeton didn't kill Michelle." I was standing in the office of the district attorney for Douglas County. He'd agreed to give me five minutes. Pretty generous considering he didn't know me from Adam, and I was trying to destroy his case. "She's gone. Why else would she disappear?"

"What do you mean, 'gone?'" DA Brown asked.

"She was scheduled to arrive in New Orleans last night at eleven thirty. My guy on the ground said she never arrived. He stayed until two o'clock, to be sure. There weren't any other flights coming in from Lincoln. My assistant, Dalton, checked the other flights leaving around that time. If she was going to New Orleans, then she would have stopped in either Atlanta or Denver. She could have gone anywhere from those two places."

"Mrs. Bridgeton wasn't required to stay in New Orleans."

"I understand that, but she said that's where she was going and lied. Why would she lie?"

"You don't know that. The woman might have changed her mind or maybe she decided to visit a friend. I'll have one of our people contact her in New Orleans in a few days."

"You won't be able to find her to testify."

"Stop worrying, Ms. Jackson. We have the guilty party waiting to post bail. And your client, Mr. Keeney, has had the murder charges dropped. Be happy. You did your job. Now go home."

"She knew about his affairs, including the ones with her sister and Kristi Briggs. My assistant found a gas receipt that puts her in Wahoo, NE, one day before Briggs was killed."

"Thank you for the information, Ms. Jackson. My office can handle the investigation from here."

Clearly, I wasn't going to convince DA Brown that he needed to take another look at Sarah Bridgeton, but that didn't mean that I had to stop looking for her. Dalton told me that he found a rental-car agreement from her last trip to New York City. From there, he was able to track a few gas receipts. Sarah wasn't as careful as she should have been. She was using one of Michelle's old credit cards. I left the office feeling a little deflated, but still determined. In my Jeep, I called Charlie.

"If your wife cheated on you with several men, what would you do?" I asked him, knowing he'd never been married, planned to get married, and loved being a bachelor.

"I'd get revenge in a heartbeat."

"Would you want to see it all play out, or would you be happy just knowing it was happening the way you thought it would?"

"There ain't nothin sweeter than seeing the look on someone's face when they figure out that you got 'em."

"That's what I was thinkin. What if Sarah didn't leave?"

"You mean like she stayed in Lincoln the whole time?"

"Yeah. That's exactly what I mean."

"She might have circled back."

I hadn't thought of that until he said it.

"She's in Omaha," I said.

"I bet she is," Charlie said. "The question for you is 'where?'"

I thanked Charlie and sent a text to Dalton asking him to check rental cars leaving Lincoln in the last twenty-four hours. While I waited for an answer, I drove to Michael Mathews' home in the Fairacres neighborhood just north of Dodge Street, in Omaha. When I phoned his office, his receptionist said that he'd returned home. If anyone knew where Sarah Bridgeton was, it would be Michael.

Michael's house sat far back from the winding road that meandered in front of his lush, well-manicured lawn. I pulled into the semicircular drive and parked. Walking the large stone steps to the expansive wood and etched glass doors reminded me how wealthy his family was. Wealthy enough to get away with murder. I rang the bell and waited. I rang it a few more times, but no one answered, so I walked around the back, hopped the fence, and began peeking into windows. I saw Michael through what must have been a window to his study. He stood with his hands slightly raised at his sides and was talking with someone.

His eyes were wide, exposing all the white around the iris. I couldn't see who he was talking to and moved to find a better vantage point. When I did, I stepped on something, setting off a series of lawn sprinklers. Michael turned to see what was happening, I ducked, and then heard a loud *pop*.

Guns have a distinct sound and once you hear it, you never forget. I drew my gun and peered over a shrub closer to the window for a better view. Michael lay bleeding on a large rug and Sarah knelt beside him, rocking. There was no way for me to assess the damage from where I was. I ran around to a side door, broke the glass to unlock it, and went inside, walking quickly past rooms until I located the study.

Sarah had taken a scarf and was applying pressure to his shoulder area. Tears dripped from her face. She'd set her gun on the floor next to Michael. When she realized I was in the room, she snatched it and pointed it in my direction. I dove behind a couch just before she squeezed off a shot.

From behind the couch, I said, "We need to call an ambulance for your brother." I'd already done that before entering the study, but she didn't need to know that. "He's losing a lot of blood." I could hear her sobbing. "Sarah, let me help you."

"No! You can't help me. And neither could Michael."

"What do you mean?"

"Michael knew. He warned me about Cal, but I didn't listen. I thought I could be the good wife and he'd change. That lying bastard deserves to go to prison."

"But he didn't kill your sister or Briggs, did he?"

"Ha! It's his fault that they're both dead."

"But he didn't do it, did he? It was you."

Sirens blaring in the distance came closer and easier to hear.

"It was so easy. He's such a fool."

I peeked around the corner of the sofa. She'd relaxed her position and Michael's breathing was labored.

"Let me check on your brother. He needs help."

She looked down at him and I rushed her, trapping her gun hand and swinging around to elbow her in the face. She released the gun, and I kicked it out of reach. When the police and ambulance arrived, I had her face-down, with her arm locked behind her back. Every time she attempted to move, I applied more pressure to her wrist. After a few tries, she gave up.

A WEEK LATER, I VISITED Michael in the hospital. The bullet had gone through his left shoulder. He had broken pieces of bone and torn tissue, but no permanent damage.

"Thank you," he said, as he tried to sit up a little higher in his hospital bed.

"Just doing my job. I'm sorry about Sarah," I said, and helped him with his pillows.

"I'm happy I stopped her from doing anything else. She was going to go after Cal."

"Did you know she killed Michelle and Kristi Briggs?" I don't know why I asked. If he did know, then he was, at the very least, on the hook as an accessory after the fact in Michelle's case.

"No, I didn't know about them. I thought Cal killed Michelle because that's what Sarah told me. She said she saw him do it and that's why she ran." No wonder he believed her. Shit, I would have believed that story. For a while.

"She confessed to killing Kristi Briggs, so the DA dropped the charges against Cal. He was released a few days ago."

"Good. Maybe he can get his life back."

"I don't know about that. Sam Myers did a real number on him."

"Great name for that holding company of his, huh?" Michael tried to laugh but winced. "I might be able to lend him a hand if he'll accept it."

My phone rang and I saw that it was Murphy. "I've got to get going. When you get out, let's do lunch." I grinned and left the room.

In the corridor on my way to the elevators, I answered my phone.

"Murphy?"

"Check the news. They're calling it the North Downing Incident."

"North Downing?"

"That's the street the arms dealer lived on. The one whose family James' team executed for the senator and Commander Earley. It's hitting the airwaves as we speak."

I stopped in the hospital lounge on the first level. The TV was tuned to CNN.

In a stunning tale of drugs, guns, and killing for hire, Senator Carmichael Richie has found himself in the center of a scandal. A press conference is scheduled for later today during which it's expected that Senator Richie will resign. The United States Attorney's office is investigating. Our sources revealed that the attorney's office received several boxes of evidence from a group calling themselves Alec Covington. Who or what Alec Covington is remains to be seen. In other news...

"Pretty damn satisfying, right?" Murphy asked.

I started walking out to the parking lot. "Only if he goes down and stays down."

"Oh, he will. There's no recovering from this level of shit storm no matter who you are."

"Where's Haithem?"

"Already back in Lincoln debriefing."

"What about Scott and Remington?"

"The less you know about that situation, the better."

"And you?"

"I'll be there tonight."

"Bring Thai and don't forget the beer."

Thank You!

IF YOU ENJOYED READING **NORTH DOWNING**, please consider leaving a review with your favorite book retailer.

Reader reviews are one of the best ways you can support the indie authors you love!

Join Sinfully Scandalous readers everywhere at www.koridmiller.com.

About the Author

KORI MILLER'S CREATIVE non-fiction and fiction has been published by Fine Lines Literary Journal. She's a freelance writer, editor, and educator who enjoys helping people reach their goals one bite-size step at a time.

Dedication, Acknowledgments, & Kudos

MY POWER AND STRENGTH come from the support and wisdom I gain from my family.

For all the badass women in the world who haven't embraced their badassery, yet.

BIG kudos to my editor, Larry Miller. A HUGE thank you to Rodney Williams for answering several technical questions and Caine Door, creator of The Adventure Frequency Network for consistently sharing my news with others.

I include the names of several real businesses in my stories. Some of them are:

Zio's Pizzeria, Orchard Hill Creamery, Pizzeria Davlo, Yia Yia's Pizza, and Brazen Head Irish Pub. These are locally owned businesses that I've supported for many years. If you're ever in Omaha or Lincoln, look them up! (Yes, like my character, Dez, I love pizza!)

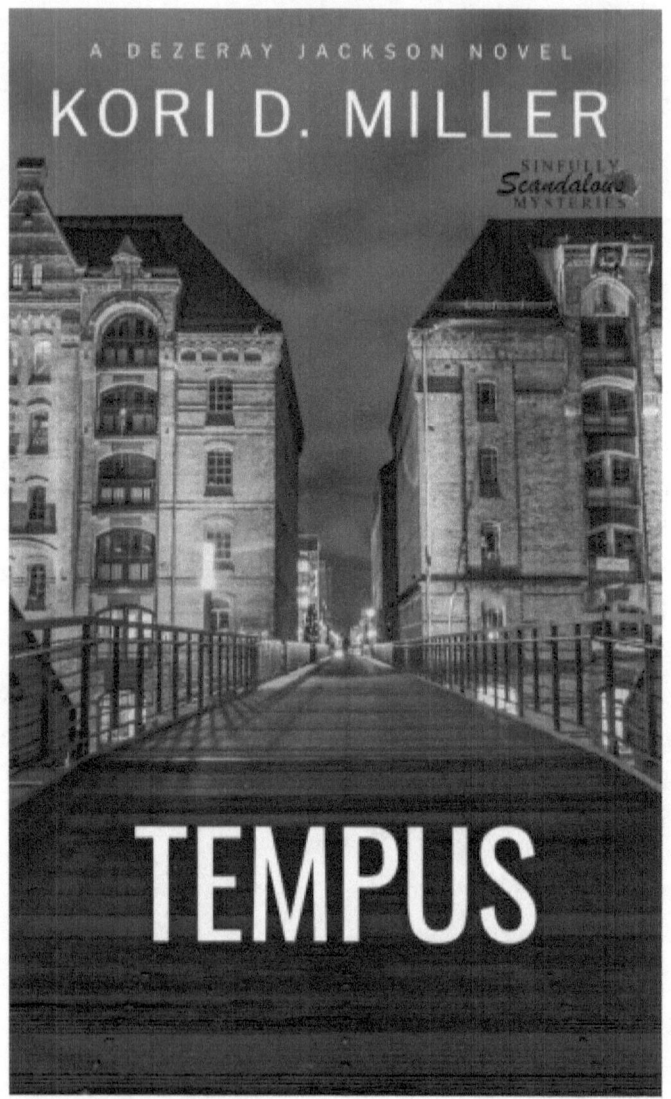

TEMPUS

DEZ IS A MAGNET FOR the downtrodden. Her Great Aunt Violet used to warn her to stay clear of broken and damaged people. But a sign on her forehead reads, "Tell me anything." And they always do.

When Dez gets cornered by a frustrated cashier asking for advice, she wants the sign to stop blinking. After a long night snapping pics for her latest case of liars and cheaters, all Dez wants is popcorn, a glass of wine, and to binge-watch something-anything. But then, the cashier's 19-year-old sister ends up dead. The police ruled the death a suicide. But the sister is unconvinced and wants Dez to find proof. The cashier's sister was dating someone, but with no name, Dez has nothing to go on. It'll take a lot of digging to find a person without a name. But if Dez does, will she find proof the sister didn't kill herself?

Don't miss out!

Visit the website below and you can sign up to receive emails whenever Kori D. Miller publishes a new book. There's no charge and no obligation.

https://books2read.com/r/B-A-OKYJ-UHRJ

Also by Kori D. Miller

A Dezeray Jackson Short Read
Deadly Sins I
Deadly Sins II
Deadly Sins III

Sinfully Scandalous Mysteries
Hush: A Dezeray Jackson Novel
North Downing: A Dezeray Jackson Novel
Tempus: A Dezeray Jackson Novel

Standalone
My Life in Black and White

Watch for more at https://www.koridmiller.com.

About the Publisher

Established in 2014, Back Porch Writer Press publishes adult, young adult, middle grade, and children's fiction and non-fiction. Our current list includes mystery, memoir, and science fiction titles.